STAIRWELL STANDOFF

Frank and Joe took the cement stairs of the high-rise office building two at a time. The *chunk-chunk-chunk* of their footsteps was answered by heavier footsteps above them.

"There's only one way to do this," said Joe, hiking himself up onto the banister.

"Go for it!" Frank replied. "I'll hop on after you!"

With a loud whoop, the Hardy brothers slid down to the first floor. When they got to the bottom, Joe hopped off and rammed his shoulder against the metal exit door.

Whomp! The sound of the impact echoed through the stairwell.

"Uh-oh," Frank muttered.

In the dim light, they could read a large metal sign that was screwed into the door. Its red letters said No Re-entry on This Floor. Go to 2.

Another sound—that of clomping feet—grew loud behind them.

They were trapped.

Books in THE HARDY BOYS CASEFILES® Series

Available from ARCHWAY Paperbacks

THE HARDY BOYS CASEFILES NO. 18

A KILLING
IN THE MARKET

FRANKLIN W. DIXON

AN ARCHWAY PAPERBACK
Published by POCKET BOOKS
New York   London   Toronto   Sydney   Tokyo   Singapore

AN ARCHWAY PAPERBACK *Original*

An Archway Paperback published by
POCKET BOOKS, a division of Simon & Schuster Inc.
1230 Avenue of the Americas, New York, NY 10020

ISBN: 0-671-68472-8

First Archway Paperback printing August 1988

10 9 8 7 6 5

Printed in the U.S.A.

IL 7+

A KILLING
IN THE MARKET

Chapter

1

"THIS IS A fine mess you got us into," Joe Hardy muttered to his brother, Frank, glancing at him over his shoulder. Joe's brow was beaded with sweat, and strands of blond hair stuck to it. Frank's dark, lean face was set in a grimace as he shifted the heavy bundles he was carrying.

The sound of laughter came from behind them. "You boys are moving like a pair of old men."

Joe craned his neck and said, "Aunt Gertrude, don't you think you kind of overdid the groceries this time?"

Gertrude Hardy smiled at the sight of her two nephews weighted down with the bags. "*You* were the ones who kept adding things! And Frank *did* volunteer your services." Her eyes twinkled mischievously as she said, "Now, don't tell me you can eat all of that but can't carry it home!"

Frank forced a chuckle, but Joe just grunted as they crossed the Bayport village square. Taking in the neat white clapboard church, the solid-looking bank, and the clean brick stores, Joe understood why his aunt preferred to shop in town. But as he counted the number of blocks they had left to walk, he vowed to himself that they'd take the van next time—and go to a supermarket with lots of parking space.

"Why don't you boys let me carry something?" Aunt Gertrude suggested. She slid the strap of her purse higher up on her right shoulder, reached out with that arm to Joe—and immediately let out a terrifying scream.

As Frank and Joe swung around, a bicyclist whooshed by them, practically knocking them over.

"My purse!" Aunt Gertrude yelled. "He's got my purse!"

Frank and Joe dropped their grocery bags, sending geysers of milk, orange juice, and tomato sauce all over the sidewalk. "We'll get him!" Frank shouted as he and his brother took off.

Ahead of them, the thief pedaled past the corner bakery and whipped into the side street, his black jacket flapping and Aunt Gertrude's purse dangling from his arm. Frank and Joe followed, already twenty yards behind him.

2

They rounded the corner into a narrow, nearly empty side street. The cyclist was halfway to the end of the block, veering to the left to avoid the only pedestrian, a gray-haired man carrying an umbrella.

The man froze, a look of mild surprise on his face as the cyclist yelled at him. "Out of my way, you old—"

"Stop, thief!" Aunt Gertrude yelled.

In a split second the gray-haired man's eyes darted from the cyclist to the brothers to Aunt Gertrude, sizing up the situation.

The cyclist whizzed past him with less than a foot to spare. But instead of jumping out of the way, the man calmly reached out with his umbrella—and thrust it between the spokes of the speeding wheels.

With a *scrrriiink,* the umbrella made contact, and the bicycle jerked into the air.

"Whooooooa!" the thief yelled, his bike flipping over and tumbling him to the street. Aunt Gertrude's purse sailed away, its contents scattering all over the pavement.

Frank and Joe ran to the thief, who was crumpled up beside the delivery entrance of the bakery, motionless. Joe grabbed a wrist to check the guy's pulse. "Alive but in dreamland," he said.

"Well, I hope they're good dreams," the older man said. "Because where he's going, it's going to be a nightmare."

The boys took in the gray-haired man standing over them completely unruffled. He looked like a sixty-year-old preppie, with pressed chino pants and cardigan sweater, his perfectly combed silver hair glinting in the afternoon sun. An early autumn tan showed that he had spent time at the beach—or under a sunlamp.

"That was quick thinking," Joe complimented him.

The man flashed a dimpled smile. "Nothing any citizen shouldn't do," he said, turning to Aunt Gertrude as she joined them. "Especially to help a charming lady."

The color rose in Aunt Gertrude's face. "I can't believe how you stopped him!" she said, breathlessly huffing and puffing. Then she knelt, gathering the things that had fallen out of her purse—change purse, cosmetics case, notebook, a gold pen.

"Here, let me help you," the silver-haired man volunteered. He knelt beside Aunt Gertrude. "Please," he said, gently touching her arm. "I'll do it."

Aunt Gertrude stood and ran her fingers through her dark hair, trying to straighten it. "Thank you so much, Mr.—er—"

"Call me Cyril," he said with a warm grin. "Cyril Bayard. And don't mention it. I work in New York City"—he chuckled—"and see bicycle messengers almost run into people on the street

4

all the time. To tell you the truth, I've been waiting a long time to pull this trick!" He patted his now-battered umbrella and winked.

As Mr. Bayard picked up some dollar bills, Aunt Gertrude said, "I should offer you some kind of a reward. At least, Mr. Bayard, I could replace your umbrella—"

"Don't worry about it," Mr. Bayard said. "I was happy that I could help. That smile is reward enough."

Gertrude Hardy looked down at the ground. Joe wasn't sure, but he thought he could see his aunt blushing.

"And, please," Mr. Bayard went on, "call me Cyril."

Joe and Frank both tried to hide a grin as they propped the thief against the side wall of the bakery. Curious passersby were gathering back at the corner, and the wail of a siren told them the police were on the way.

The crowd parted as a squad car screeched around the corner and skidded to a stop beside the four. As the front door swung open, a familiar stocky form in blue stepped out.

A grin lit up Con Riley's beefy features as he took in the scene. "Heads-up work, boys," Officer Riley said, leaning down to examine the thief's face. "We've had a lot of complaints about this guy."

"We didn't do anything," Frank answered modestly. "It's all because of Mr. Bayard—"

He and Joe turned around, expecting Mr. Bayard to accept the compliment. But his back was to them, his arm resting casually against the building. He was laughing in response to something Aunt Gertrude had said, and she was smiling broadly.

Officer Riley's partner helped the groggy thief stumble into the cruiser while he took statements from the boys, Aunt Gertrude, and Mr. Bayard. When he had all the answers he needed, Officer Riley slid back into the car and drove off.

"What now?" Joe asked. The passersby had straggled away, but Aunt Gertrude and Mr. Bayard showed no sign of moving. As she laughed at something Mr. Bayard said, Aunt Gertrude's face seemed younger than Joe could remember it—softer, almost vulnerable.

"Let's go get the stuff we dropped," Frank suggested quietly.

The grocery bags were where they had left them, torn and soaked with milk and juice.

"Can you believe what we were watching?" Joe asked as they started scooping up everything.

"I think she's really falling for that guy," Frank answered, shaking his head.

"Yeah. You know, somehow it's hard for me to imagine Aunt Gertrude actually in love. I mean, she's too *old* for that."

"I'll tell her you said so." Frank laughed as Joe feigned sudden terror. Then he got a little more serious. "I'm sure it's happened before— probably years ago. Besides, you know what she's always saying to Dad—"

"Right." Joe did a perfect imitation of Aunt Gertrude's voice: " 'I tell you, Fenton, I'd kill for a nice older millionaire to sweep me off my feet.' "

The boys kept on working to salvage as many groceries as they could. Frank tossed one bagful of empty milk and juice cartons into a trash basket, then said, "Look on the bright side. We've got a lot less to carry."

As they went back around the corner, they saw Aunt Gertrude and Mr. Bayard scanning the ground.

"There were some things we missed." Aunt Gertrude leaned down to snatch up a pair of knitting needles and put them into her purse. "Knitting is my dearest hobby." She looked Mr. Bayard up and down and smiled shyly. "Sweaters are my specialty, you know. In fact, I have some beautiful cashmere yarn at home—"

Mr. Bayard laughed. "Don't go to any trouble." Then he reached for a small booklet spread open on the sidewalk. "Is this yours?" he asked, looking at it curiously. "A savings account passbook. I haven't seen one of these in years!"

7

"I've kept it faithfully since I was a little girl. My life savings is in it."

Bayard shook his head. "My dear, you live in the Stone Age!" he said with a laugh. "Aren't you aware of more sophisticated investments—mutual funds, tax-free municipal bonds—"

Aunt Gertrude gave him a sheepish look. "No, I really don't know much about any of those things—is that bad?"

"It's not my business to tell you that you've probably lost an opportunity to make a lot of money." He smiled. "Well, actually it *is* my business. I'm an investment counselor—semi-retired. I still keep an office in New York."

"How fascinating! Maybe you could give me some advice!"

Mr. Bayard chuckled and said, "Well, usually I deal only with multimillion-dollar corporations, but I wouldn't mind *one* personal client—"

"Um, Aunt Gertrude," Joe said, "ready to go home?"

Aunt Gertrude greeted Joe with a broad smile. "Frank, Joe, this is Cyril Bayard. He's kindly offered to help us carry the groceries home. Isn't that nice of him?"

With a gallant gesture, Mr. Bayard grabbed the lightest grocery bag, the only one that hadn't ripped. Together they walked along the tree-shaded residential blocks back to the Hardy house.

"Why don't you come for dinner?" Aunt Gertrude said. "My brother, Fenton, and his wife have just left for a month's vacation, and I've been cooking for the boys." She turned to Frank and Joe. "You wouldn't mind, would you, boys?"

"Uh, no." Frank looked at Joe.

"Of course not," Joe said.

"Thanks," Mr. Bayard said. "I'd love to come. Do you follow the market?" He started talking about things like no-load futures and growth-and-income securities. Turning to Aunt Gertrude, he said, "If you're really interested, I could look into some secure investments for you."

"Oh, I'm interested, all right," she said. But as he trudged home, Joe couldn't help wondering whether her interest was in finance or in Cyril Bayard. And was Mr. Bayard's interest romantic or something else? He seemed pretty eager to get his hands on Aunt Gertrude's money. . . .

That evening Aunt Gertrude made Mr. Bayard a delicious pasta dinner. Tuesday it was fried chicken, and on Wednesday an entire leg of lamb.

"Mmmmm-mmmm," said Joe during the after-dinner cleanup. "Looks like Aunt Gertrude's going to get to Mr. Bayard's heart through his stomach."

"She's serious about him," Frank agreed.

"She's sure doing some serious cooking," Joe said. "I can hardly wait for dinner tomorrow."

But when they got home for dinner on Thursday, there was no sign of Aunt Gertrude—or of Mr. Bayard.

"Hmmm," Joe mused. "Maybe she left something for us."

But after checking the oven and the fridge, they realized that dinner hadn't been prepared.

"I'm starving," Joe said. "What do you say to pizza?"

Frank shook his head. "Let's hang out a few minutes." He frowned. "This isn't like Aunt Gertrude. She'd have left us a note. Maybe she went someplace with Mr. Bayard, and they got delayed."

They spent an uncomfortable half hour pretending not to be worried and peering out into the gathering dusk. But Gertrude Hardy was nowhere to be seen.

At eight o'clock Joe's stomach began to growl. "You think she's at Mr. Bayard's?" he asked.

"I don't know. Let's call," Frank suggested.

"He's unlisted. I had the same idea a few minutes ago."

"Well, that leaves us one choice, doesn't it?" Frank began heading for the front door. "Now we know how she feels when we don't come home on time."

Joe followed him outside, and they both climbed into their black van. The tires squealed as Frank backed out of the driveway and followed the same route to Mr. Bayard's cottage that they'd used to drive him home on Monday.

A mist was rolling in off the bay as Frank and Joe stopped in front of a small, gray-shingled bungalow. A flickering amber light in the living room window shone out into the darkness.

"Fire!" Joe bolted out of the van, followed by Frank. They ran toward the house and pulled themselves up onto the ledge of the window.

Then they both lowered themselves down again.

They had seen a fire all right. Cyril Bayard had been fanning it in his fireplace while Aunt Gertrude rhythmically moved back and forth in a rocking chair, busily knitting a sweater. In a corner a parrot preened itself in its cage.

"Home sweet home," Joe muttered. "She's forgotten about us!"

"Let's not spoil her good time," Frank said. "We can go home and order a pizza."

Joe nodded. "Guess we're lucky they didn't see us. It would have been embarrassing."

They started to creep silently back to their van, which they could barely make out in the gray of the moonless evening.

But before they hit the front sidewalk, Frank suddenly gasped. There was no mistaking the gleaming object that had been thrust in front of his face—the muzzle of a revolver.

Chapter

2

"DON'T JUST STOP like tha—" Joe didn't have time to finish his sentence before he saw what had stopped his brother. He gaped at the .38.

Silently, they threw up their hands and backed slowly into the diffused light from the living room window. Focusing on the gun, all they saw *was* the gun—along with a man's wrist jutting out of an expensive silk shirt. Joe just took in a letter *S* on his cuff link when the living room window was thrown up with a loud screech. "What's going on out there?" a voice called out.

The brothers spun around. Their aunt Gertrude was leaning out and looking around.

And slowly, a low chuckling began. Frank and Joe stared in confusion at their assailant as he put his gun down and stepped directly into the rectangle of light from the window.

"Mr. Bayard!" Frank said, lowering his arms in relief.

"Frank? Frank, is that you?" Aunt Gertrude asked.

"It's all right, Gertrude!" Mr. Bayard called out. "Just your nephews!" He smiled at Frank and Joe. "Sorry, boys. I heard some noise and thought there were prowlers—so I sneaked out to get the drop on them."

"Oh, my heavens!" Aunt Gertrude said, letting out a sigh of relief.

"Is life always this exciting around the Hardy family?" Mr. Bayard said, chuckling. "I moved to Bayport because my doctor told me my heart needed less work and more rest."

Aunt Gertrude looked at Frank and Joe and shook her finger. "You see how dangerous it is when you go poking around, playing detective? You could have given Cyril a heart attack—not to mention that you could have gotten killed if Cyril used that gun!"

"Sorry, Aunt Gertrude," Joe said. By now he and Frank had gotten used to Aunt Gertrude's calling what they did "playing detective." Although her brother, Fenton, had been a detective all his life, Aunt Gertrude had never been comfortable with his dangerous line of work. She definitely didn't think it was appropriate for Fenton's sons.

"It's all right, Gertrude," Mr. Bayard said. "Why don't I bring them inside for some hot cider and we'll all calm down and laugh about it."

But Aunt Gertrude was still annoyed as Mr. Bayard ushered Frank and Joe inside. "Why didn't you boys just knock?"

Frank smiled. "We saw the flickering light and came to fight a fire. And—well, we saw that you were having such a good time, and we didn't want to disturb you—"

"Really, we can fend for ourselves for dinner," Joe added.

Aunt Gertrude's eyes widened. She glanced at her watch. "Oh, my goodness—dinner! I completely lost track of time. Please forgive me, boys. Here I am yelling at you, when I was the one who didn't show up to cook!" She bustled across the room to get her coat from the closet. "You'll have to excuse me, Cyril. I must be going! You don't mind if I leave my knitting bag here, do you?"

"Aunt Gertrude, it's all right! You can stay," Frank insisted. "We'll make something for ourselves, or—"

"Oh, don't be silly. The only thing you'd make is a mess of the kitchen," Aunt Gertrude shot back. She tucked her purse under her arm. Walking toward the door, she paused before Mr. Bayard and smiled shyly. "I—I had a wonderful time, Cyril," she said.

Both Mr. Bayard and Aunt Gertrude gave the brothers sidelong glances. Frank nudged Joe in the ribs and said, "We're out of here."

As Frank and Joe walked out to the van, the two adults lingered in the cottage doorway, talking in soft voices.

"Bet they haven't had so much fun in thirty years," Joe remarked.

Frank gave his brother an accusing look and stifled a laugh. "What a rotten nephew," he said.

A moment later Aunt Gertrude headed down the walk to the van, and the three of them were on their way home. As they drove along, Aunt Gertrude kept staring absentmindedly out the window. The only sounds in the van were occasional rumblings of hunger from Joe's stomach.

"You're awfully quiet, Aunt Gertrude," Frank finally said as they stopped for a traffic light.

Aunt Gertrude smiled. "Just feeling thoughtful, I suppose—"

Joe laughed. "You really like that guy, don't you?"

"Well, I guess so. He's a gentleman, he's well educated . . ." Aunt Gertrude looked around and saw that her nephews were all ears. "And if it will stop you two from snooping around, I'll come out and tell you. Yes, I happen to like Cyril very much. I can't tell you how wonderful it is for a woman of my age to meet a man like him. Not only is he interested in everything about me, but he's—unattached.''

Joe raised an eyebrow. "A bachelor? At his age?''

"No, Joseph! If you *must* know, Cyril is divorced.''

"Well, I think you made a good catch, Aunt Gertrude—a stockbroker,'' Joe said lightly.

"As a matter of fact, Cyril works for Colt Fadiman—one of the most prestigious investment companies in New York City,'' Gertrude told him. "We've been talking about investing my savings.''

"Uh-oh,'' Joe told her. "Are you sure he's not after your fortune?''

Aunt Gertrude gave him a look. "If I were you, I wouldn't joke about fifty thousand dollars.''

Frank let out a whistle. "Not bad, Aunt Gertrude!''

Gertrude Hardy smiled proudly. "Well, I worked all those years when I was younger, and I managed to save a bit for a rainy day.''

Frank's voice was quiet as he broke in. "If you've saved that much money, are you sure you want a near stranger taking charge of it?''

"Cyril is not a stranger, Joe. Besides, anyone who works for Colt Fadiman—''

"Did he tell you exactly how he was going to invest it?" Joe asked.

"Well, not exactly, but he said to let him worry about it. Something about capital something-or-other securities—"

Joe tried to hold in his disbelief. "Aunt Gertrude, I don't mean to be disrespectful, but you barely know the guy, and you have no idea where your life savings are about to end up. I mean, the papers are full of stories about swindlers—guys who work for these big-and-mighty companies and steal clients' money left and right!"

"Joseph, I will not hear another word of this! Cyril is as honest a man as I've ever met, and I have the utmost confidence in his intentions!"

"I'm sure Joe just meant you might want to start off in small chunks—maybe ten thousand or so," Frank suggested.

Gertrude shook her head. "I've already promised Cyril the full amount—changing things now would make it seem as if I didn't trust him."

"And you're sure you want to trust him . . ." Frank shrugged. They rode in silence for the rest of the ride.

"What's wrong with it?" Callie Shaw asked as she parked her car in front of the Hardy house. "I mean, she's a perfectly attractive woman!"

"Cyril Bayard certainly thinks Aunt Gertrude

is attractive.'' Frank laughed. "But I have other ideas about what makes a woman attractive.''

Callie tossed back her medium-length blond hair and smiled at Frank. "Want to share your ideas?'' She drew her face to within inches of Frank's and closed her eyes expectantly.

"Well, to start—'' Frank answered. He wrapped his arms around her and touched his lips to hers.

Honnnnk! A sudden blast broke the spell. With a start Frank and Callie pulled away from each other.

"What the—'' Frank said angrily. He turned and was confronted by a shiny black slab, which he immediately recognized as the side of the Hardy van.

"I see you in there,'' Joe's voice rang out. "Even though the windows are all steamy.''

Callie slumped back into her seat.

"Sorry, Callie,'' Frank said. He stuck his head out the window and called, "Thanks, Joe, for the ride home from Callie's house! If I'd waited for you, I'd still be there.''

"Doesn't look like you minded *too* much!'' Joe answered with a grin.

They were interrupted just then by a strangled-sounding scream from inside their house.

"Trouble!'' Joe burst from the van, tearing for the house. Callie threw open her door and started running, too, closely followed by Frank.

"Hope this isn't like the last time we dashed to the rescue," Frank muttered.

It was. They found Aunt Gertrude standing in the middle of the kitchen, trembling. On the floor, splattered around and on her, was a huge mound of spaghetti with red clam sauce.

"What happened?" Frank asked. "I thought you were having dinner with Mr. Bayard tonight."

Aunt Gertrude looked furious. "That's what I thought too," she said through tight lips. "Five o'clock. That's what he said. It's almost six. But is he here yet? No!"

"Is this what you were going to serve him?" Joe asked, looking at the mess.

"No, we were going out! But I was going to whip together a little something for you and Frank. And now look what happened. He's got me so angry—"

Frank thought back. It had been a rocky two weeks since Aunt Gertrude had started seeing Mr. Bayard. At first everything had gone smoothly, but lately Mr. Bayard had stood her up a couple of times. Even though his excuses had always been good, Aunt Gertrude was beginning to feel hurt.

"Oh, I was so mad at him last week. And then—" Her eyes began to water, and she turned away from her nephews. "Then we took a nice walk last night, and everything seemed fine."

"Maybe he was called in to his office, like that day last week," Frank suggested. "They may still be in."

He went to the phone, got the number for Colt Fadiman from Information, and called Mr. Bayard's office.

"Colt Fadiman, Mr. Bayard's line," a cheerful voice answered.

"Hello, may I speak to him, please?"

"I'm sorry, Mr. Bayard is on vacation."

"Uh—yes. But is there any chance that he might have come in today?"

The person at the other end chuckled. "Oh, I doubt it. He's been touring Europe for the past few months—"

"Thank y— Wait a minute, did you say Europe?"

"Yes, sir. Until at least December first. May I leave a message?"

Thinking fast, Frank asked, "Well, uh, maybe you can help me. I met several investment counselors at the, uh—convention last month, and I'm not sure I have the correct person. Is Mr. Bayard a tall, thin, gray-haired gentleman?"

"Oh, no, sir," the other voice chortled. "Mr. Bayard would be so flattered. To tell the truth, he doesn't have much hair left, and he's only five foot seven—and rather, how should I say, heavy-set—"

"I see," Frank said. "Well, I guess I must have gotten his business card mixed up with someone else's. Thank you."

"What was that all about?" Joe asked after his brother hung up.

Frank tapped his fingers on the kitchen table. "Something's very wrong here. The secretary's description didn't match Mr. Bayard at all."

"What?" Aunt Gertrude said. "I don't understand."

"Let's go pay *our* Mr. Bayard a little visit."

Once again they took the route along Bay Road to Mr. Bayard's place. The cottage was pitch-dark. Frank grabbed a flashlight from the glove compartment, and he and Joe helped Aunt Gertrude and Callie out. The four of them walked silently toward the front door.

"Not even a porch light," Aunt Gertrude whispered. "Maybe he did spend the day in New York City."

Frank flicked on the light and boosted himself up to peer in through the front window. "Well, wherever he went, it doesn't look like he'll be back for a while."

Joe raised himself up and pushed his face against the window. As Frank shone the beam around, Joe was stunned.

It looked as if the entire living room had been

torn apart. The armchair where Aunt Gertrude had sat was on its side, the cover slashed to reveal the stuffing underneath.

The rug was rolled back, and even the logs from the fireplace had been rolled out.

There was no sign of Cyril Bayard.

Chapter

3

"SQUAAWWWWK! BUY LOW, sell high! Bull market! No sweat! Squaawwwwk!"

After Frank pried open the front door, the screeching of the parrot greeted them. It was the only sound in Mr. Bayard's living room. To the left, the couch had undergone the same slashing routine as the chair. Several wooden planks had been ripped out of the floor where the rug had been taken up.

"What happened to Cyril?" Aunt Gertrude murmured, her face frozen with shock.

"I'll call the police," Joe said. He went to look for the phone while Frank tried to comfort his aunt. "Easy now," Frank said. "We'll get to the bottom of this."

"Dinner? No sweat! Brrrock!" the parrot called out.

"I—I think he's hungry," Aunt Gertrude said listlessly. Frank followed her into the kitchen and over to a cupboard. Her face looked pale and drained. With shaking hands she reached into one of the cabinets and pulled out a box of birdseed. But as she was lowering it to the countertop, she abruptly lost her grip. The seed spilled noisily onto the floor.

"Oh, no!" she cried.

"It's okay! I'll pick it up!" Frank said.

"No, no, it's not that, Frank. Look!" With an expression of horror she pointed to the counter-top. On it was a copy of *The New York Times* from the week before, folded open to a story. Frank picked it up and read the headline.

WALL STREET CLERK SHOT
MISTAKEN FOR BOSS BY GUNMAN?

And then Frank saw what had upset Aunt Gertrude so much. Below the headline was a smiling photo of Mr. Bayard in a jacket and tie with the caption *Henry Simone*.

"Henry Simone?" Frank muttered.

"Wh-what does it say, Frank?" Aunt Gertrude asked.

He read aloud.

"Yesterday evening, after business hours, a gunman gained access to the offices of the investment firm Thompson Welles. The intruder used a heavy-caliber pistol to fire three shots into Peter Lance, an assistant to executive Henry Simone. Mr. Lance died immediately.

The assailant escaped the building before the body was found. Police suspect that the attacker mistook the clerk for Henry Simone, an investment counselor of great notoriety in Manhattan finance. . . ."

By this time Joe had returned and was listening intently. "Sounds like old Cyril—or should we call him Henry—had a bit of trouble back home," he said.

Frank paced back and forth. "Obviously, somebody's after him, and he knew it. Otherwise why would he skip to Bayport using the name of someone he knew was going to be out of the country for a while?"

"When exactly did this shooting happen?" Joe asked.

Frank looked at the top of the newspaper. "Last Friday."

"That was just about the time he started acting weird around Aunt Gertrude."

Aunt Gertrude knelt down to gather up the

birdseed. "I don't believe this has happened," she said, standing up again.

"Look on the bright side, Aunt Gertrude," Joe said. "There are no bullet holes, no bloodstains. Maybe Cyril—or Simone, or whatever his name is—is still alive."

Aunt Gertrude looked as if she were about to faint. "Bullet holes—bloodstains?"

"Nice work—really sympathetic," Frank said to Joe under his breath. He took his aunt by the arm and led her out of the kitchen to a seat near the dining room table, where she had left one of her knitting bags a week and a half earlier.

Just then the wail of a police siren sliced through the air. Joe went to the front door to let in Officer Riley and his partner.

"We found the place like this, but we don't know for sure what happened," Joe said. He handed Officer Riley the newspaper article. "But we did turn this up."

Officer Riley glanced at the article and surveyed the room. "Whew," he said. "I remember when stockbrokers led quiet, respectable lives."

"Whee-oo! Stockbroker, what a joker! Hey, no sweat!" the parrot squawked.

"Aah, pipe down before we book you," Officer Riley said with a smile. He took a look at the paper.

"Say, that's the fellow who stopped the cyclist

thief!'' Officer Riley's eyes narrowed. "Any of you know much about this guy?"

Frank and Joe looked at Aunt Gertrude, who was fingering a knitting needle nervously. "I do, Officer Riley," she said. "At least I thought I did—"

Officer Riley sat opposite her at the table. "Yes, I remember you talking to him."

Aunt Gertrude's worried look gave way to a deep frown. "I talked, but I guess I didn't ask the right questions," she said almost to herself. "I was fooled. I—I thought he was interested in me. But I guess my nephews were right. He wanted my money, the slimy, conniving—"

"A shame, Miss Hardy, a shame," Officer Riley interjected, shaking his head. "But if you'd just give me some facts about the man—"

"Some facts . . ." Aunt Gertrude looked up at Officer Riley with bitter, hurt eyes. "The *facts* are that Mr. Henry Simone, alias Cyril Bayard, alias who-knows-what-else, swindled a woman's life savings, everything she had. Those"—she got up from the table and started pacing—"those are the facts, Officer Riley." Aunt Gertrude had turned her face away so Officer Riley couldn't see the tears that were forming in her eyes.

"Miss Hardy," Officer Riley said gently, "we may be able to find him, if you cooperate—"

"Good! Because if you do find him—that is, if he's still alive—then bring him to me right away.

And I'll kill him!" She jabbed her magenta knitting needle in the air for emphasis.

There was an uncomfortable silence. Then all at once Aunt Gertrude turned red with embarrassment. "Oh! Oh, what am I saying?" She sank back into her chair. "I'm so sorry, Officer! Of course I didn't mean that!"

"Not to worry, ma'am," Officer Riley said with a jovial smile. "You're upset and confused. We'll talk about this some other time."

After Officer Riley and his partner finished their report, they picked up the parrot to take it to the station house for safekeeping. Frank and Joe took their aunt home. For the rest of the evening they tried to patch up Aunt Gertrude's hurt feelings.

The next morning Joe sneaked quietly down the stairs to the kitchen. His aunt had looked so exhausted the night before that he didn't want to wake her.

As he moved toward the kitchen, he imagined he could smell the bacon he was about to cook.

Suddenly a voice called out, "Don't bother sneaking around. I'm up."

Joe entered the kitchen to see Aunt Gertrude sitting at the table in her bathrobe, nibbling on a piece of crisp bacon. "Help yourself," she said, pushing a plate of bacon his way. "How would you like your eggs?"

"How did you know I was going to come down just now?" Joe asked.

Aunt Gertrude gave him a sad smile. "I woke up at three this morning and couldn't get back to sleep."

The phone rang just then. "I'll get it up here!" came Frank's voice from upstairs.

"Can't get Bayard—Simone, I mean—out of your mind, huh, Aunt Gertrude?" Joe said.

"Not to mention my money." Aunt Gertrude sighed. "I feel like such a fool."

Before Joe could answer, the rhythmic thumping of footsteps interrupted him from behind.

"Get your jacket, Joe! We've got to move!" Frank called out.

"Wha— Wait a second! I haven't eaten! What's going on?"

"That was Callie on the phone. She says she saw ten cop cars swarming around the pier as she was driving to school. She couldn't tell what's happening, but thought we'd like to check it out."

Joe bolted up out of his chair. "Sorry, Aunt Gertrude," he said, giving her a peck on the cheek. "We'll talk later, okay?"

Before she could answer, Frank and Joe were out of the house and into the van. Frank threw it into gear, and they took off to the pier.

As soon as they reached Bay Road, they spotted the revolving roof lights of the cruisers reflecting off the surrounding houses. A crowd of people stood behind a barricade of wooden sawhorses, stretching to see what was going on.

"Over here, guys!" Callie's voice rang out. Frank and Joe pulled into a space and ran to her. "Officer Riley's here. I'm sure if you tell him that I'm with you, he'll—"

Frank rolled his eyes. "Callie, I don't even know if he'll let *us* in."

"Sure, Frank, sure. This is the thanks I get for tipping you off? See if I ever help you again!"

Frank sighed. "Let's go talk to the man."

"Great!" Callie said, following them as they slid between two sawhorses.

The three of them were at the foot of the pier when they met Officer Riley, who waved them on. At the far end of the pier a group of police officers was gathered, watching a team of divers search beneath the dock.

Callie dodged excitedly left and right between the police officers to get a better view.

Frank and Joe worked their way up to the railing and looked down into the dark water.

Both brothers' jaws fell open as they saw what one surfacing diver was holding.

The body of Henry Simone—with a magenta-colored knitting needle stuck into his chest.

Chapter

4

CALLIE SHUDDERED AND turned her head away. "How horrible!"

Frank couldn't do much more than nod sadly as two police officers lifted the body over the railing and gently placed it on the ground. Around them, onlookers buzzed noisily. Police officers, led by Officer Riley, surrounded the body.

"Come on, Frank," Joe said, walking toward Officer Riley.

Frank looked back at Callie, who waved at him to go ahead without her. He joined his brother in looking over Officer Riley's shoulder.

"How long was he under, Con?" Frank asked.

"Oh, a day or so," he said.

"How did you know a body was down there?" Joe wanted to know.

"Received an anonymous tip early this morning," Con Riley answered, his mind obviously on something else.

Frank and Joe nodded solemnly, and Officer Riley looked away from them before speaking. "Uh—your aunt Gertrude," he finally said hesitantly. "Sounded to me as if she really wanted revenge on this fellow for swindling her."

"Well, she was angry," Joe replied. "I mean, she thought he was—"

Frank cut him off. "Why ask?"

Officer Riley turned back to face them and silently pointed to the bloodstained magenta knitting needle.

Joe stared at the policeman. "Wait a second! You mean, you think that Aunt Gertrude actually—"

Officer Riley shrugged his shoulders. "Obviously, I can't accuse anybody, but—well, you know, fellas, I've got to start this homicide investigation somewhere."

Frank and Joe exchanged disbelieving glances. "But, Officer Riley, how could you possibly suspect—I mean, of all the unlikely—of course she couldn't have done this—" Joe sputtered.

Officer Riley shook his head. "I'm sorry, boys, I'm going to have to ask you to bring her into the station for questioning. After school will be soon enough." He began walking to his squad car.

"No way!" Joe replied indignantly.

Officer Riley turned around. "If you don't," he said gently, "I will." He took in Joe's mutinous glare. "And, boys—I don't want her to know what evidence we've found—understand?"

That afternoon, right after school at two o'clock, Frank drove the van to the police station with his aunt in the back seat with Callie. Aunt Gertrude was nervously clutching the newspaper article about Henry Simone. "I still don't believe he's—" Her lips began quivering.

"Such a waste," Callie remarked, putting an arm around Aunt Gertrude.

"And now they want to talk to me? I don't understand this at all. Couldn't you have *told* them I'm not a murderer?"

"We all know you're not a murderer, Aunt Gertrude," Joe said. "This is more or less a formality. You'll chat with Con Riley, answer a few questions, and that'll be it!"

"I do appreciate your coming along," Aunt Gertrude told Callie as they drove into downtown Bayport. "I'd like to ask a favor though—could you please wait in the van while we go in to take care of this? It's family business."

They parked in the village square near the brick station house, leaving Callie in the van muttering about Hardys. The desk officer called Con Riley, who escorted them to his battered gray steel desk. "Would you like some tea, Miss Hardy?" he asked.

"No, thank you," Aunt Gertrude said stiffly as she sat on a wooden chair facing the policeman. "I understand you have some questions, and I'd like my nephews—whom you know so well—to stay with me. I—I'm feeling a bit fragile this afternoon."

"Fine, Miss Hardy, fine," Officer Riley said, forcing a smile. "Sit, all of you." He paced slowly across the worn green linoleum floor. "I want you to realize that my questions in no way accuse you of any wrongdoing. I'm only collecting information."

Aunt Gertrude nodded silently.

Officer Riley walked behind his desk and pulled a plastic bag with a magenta knitting needle in it out of a drawer. "Now, does this look familiar to you?"

Aunt Gertrude swallowed hard as she took it and turned it around in her hands. "Yes," she said in a parched-sounding voice. "It's like some I have."

"It seems to me that it's an unusual color, and you were holding one just like it yesterday. Is that true?"

Aunt Gertrude looked confused. "Well, yes . . ."

"Can you produce your set?" Con wanted to know.

"Well, no, I can't. I—um—seem to have mislaid one," Aunt Gertrude said, her gaze quickly flicking up to take in both her nephews.

"Mm-hmm. Now, when exactly was the last time you saw Mr. Simone?"

"We went for a long walk the night before last. Please, you're not going to ask what we talked about, are you?"

"No, Miss Hardy. Just tell me where exactly you went on this walk."

"Well, we started at the cottage and walked along Bay Road."

"Did you walk along Bay Road into town—or did you go the other way, toward the fishing pier?"

"Officer Riley," Aunt Gertrude said uncomfortably, "I don't see how any of this is your business. And I will thank you to stop asking me any more questions."

The room fell deathly silent. To change the subject, Frank asked, "Have you found Simone's next of kin?"

Officer Riley shook his head quickly. "We're still tracking them down. Let me call my contact in the New York City Police Department—he may have found someone by now." He punched the number on the phone.

As Con Riley spoke into the phone, Aunt Gertrude leaned in to Frank and Joe. "I don't think this is right!"

Frank nodded his head reassuringly. "Just do your best to answer the questions, that's all he can ask."

"All right. We've got our info," Officer Riley announced. "His only kin is a former wife who lives in Cliffside Heights—Four seventy-seven Archer Street." He raised his eyebrows as he mentioned the wealthy section of Bayport. "An expensive address. She must have had a generous alimony settlement, or she's doing well in her business."

"Which is?" Joe asked.

"She owns a restaurant here in Bayport—the Shore Inn—down on Bay Road." Riley punched more numbers on the phone. "Well, here goes. I have to make an appointment to speak to her in person. I hate informing next of kin. It's the hardest part of my job."

He paused as the phone rang at the other end. "Hello, this is Officer Riley at the Bayport police station. Uh, it's about two-thirty in the afternoon. Please call me as soon as possible." He left the phone number and hung up, explaining, "Her answering machine."

"Officer, please, may I go now?" Aunt Gertrude was almost pleading.

Con Riley sat down behind his desk, leaning forward on his elbows. "Well, actually, Miss Hardy, I still have a few things I'd like to ask you. And if you don't mind, I'll have to request that your nephews leave the room briefly." He gave Frank and Joe a sharp look.

"Fine," Frank said. "Let's go."

Aunt Gertrude sat stony-faced as they headed out the door.

As soon as they were outside the office, Joe grabbed his brother. "How could you agree to leave her alone like that?"

"Look, we both know that Aunt Gertrude has nothing to do with this. And the only other connection to Simone that we know about is his wife. Listen, I'm going to go to the Shore Inn to see if Simone's ex-wife is there. Maybe I can find out something."

"But what about Aunt Gertrude?" Joe asked.

"You stay here. This shouldn't take me long."

Joe nodded, and Frank dashed out the door and down the station steps. He opened the door to the van—to confront a smiling Callie Shaw.

"Something very interesting must be up to make you move this fast," she said.

Her eyes sparkled with excitement as he quickly explained what was up. "I'm coming with you!" she said.

"Aunt Gertrude asked—" Frank began, but Callie put her hand over his mouth.

"Aunt Gertrude asked me to stay with the van. So if you take it, I have to go with you."

"If that isn't the strangest reasoning," Frank

said. Then he gave her a big smile. "Come on, partner. Let's go."

The ride to the Shore Inn took Frank and Callie down Bay Road, the route that went past Henry Simone's cottage.

"Simone lived around here, didn't he?" Callie asked, peering out the window.

"In the clearing just past these trees," Frank said, keeping his eyes firmly on the road as it twisted left and right.

"You mean that gray cottage with the big Lincoln parked in the drive?"

Frank nodded. "That's it," he said.

Screeeech! Frank stomped on the brakes. "Lincoln parked in the drive? Simone didn't have a Lincoln. He drove a BMW. What's it doing there?"

Callie's eyes beamed with excitement. "I don't know! Let's find out!"

Frank threw the van into reverse and backed down the road, stopping just before the cottage so the van would be hidden by the trees.

Callie said, "I'm sure you've noticed this already, Frank, but there's a window open on the side of the house."

She was wrong—he hadn't noticed it. "Uh, good observation, Callie. That'll be my point of entry."

"Why don't you just knock?" Callie wanted to know.

"Because whoever's here has entered illegally. The house was sealed by the police. No one should be in it."

Before Frank could say anything else, Callie was out of the van and running beside him to the open window.

"Look," Frank whispered to her. "Nobody's in the car, so they're probably in the house. Look around downstairs; I'll take the second floor. I didn't go up there when Con did yesterday. If there's trouble, get out."

"Right."

Frank gave her a leg up and then climbed in himself. The place looked exactly as it did when they had left it.

Leaving Callie to snoop around downstairs, Frank stole silently up the stairs to the second floor. There were three doors opening off the hall. One of them was ajar. Hugging the wall, Frank sneaked over to the open door. He reached out and slowly pushed it all the way open. The hinges let out an agonizing screech.

Frank peered into the shadowy room. A queen-size mattress had been thrown off its box spring and torn to shreds. Empty drawers hung open from two dressers, and clothes were strewn around the floor.

Inside the room, he noticed a sophisticated-looking camera standing on a tripod in one corner. It appeared to be completely intact, untouched by whoever had ransacked the room.

Frank walked closer to examine it. Simone must have spent a lot on the camera, but he wasn't much of a photographer, Frank thought. Trees kept the room in shade most of the day. He would have needed a flash attachment to work in here even during the afternoon.

And what could he have been taking pictures of? Frank walked behind the camera, putting his eye up to the viewfinder.

"Go ahead, take a shot," came a low voice from behind him. "Then it'll be my turn."

Frank froze as he felt a cold metal object being pressed up against the back of his neck.

Chapter

5

"SOMEHOW, I DON'T think that's a camera you're pointing at me." Frank was amazed at how steady his voice sounded. He had to keep this guy talking until he could figure out a way to turn the tables and get the drop on him.

The only answer he got was a sharp *click*. The sound of a revolver being cocked.

But the muzzle of the gun was removed from his neck. "Turn around," his captor ordered.

Frank turned to face a tall, stocky man with a receding hairline. He wore an expensive and elegant dark blue suit. In his hand was a .38 revolver.

"Next comes the line from all the detective movies you've ever seen," the man told him.

Frank raised his hands in the air, staring at the gun.

"Good. You figured that one out. Now, how about telling me exactly why you're snooping around here, young man?"

"I was about to ask you the same question," Frank said boldly. "Do you make a habit of hiding with a gun in the closet of a house that doesn't belong to you?"

"What makes you think this house doesn't belong to me?" the man snapped.

"I think you know why," Frank said carefully. "And I think you know something about Henry Simone's death—don't you?"

The man raised one corner of his mouth in a lopsided smirk. "Something tells me we need to talk." He waved the gun toward the door. "Move."

Frank walked slowly out the door and down the stairs, followed closely by the stranger. His mind raced, searching for a way to signal Callie, to warn her.

But it wasn't necessary. Looking around the first floor of the cottage, he noticed no sign of her. She must have heard them upstairs.

"Keep moving," the man ordered. "Out the back door."

The gunman kicked the back door open and held it as Frank walked through. Parked in back of the cottage was a black BMW—Simone's car.

"Around to the side," the man said. "Get in the Lincoln, we're going for a ride. *Ugh!*"

"What did you say?" Frank asked, spinning around to see the gunman on his knees, clutching at his throat. Behind him, Callie was holding tightly to a garden hose she had thrown around his neck.

Without missing a beat Frank unleashed a karate kick to the man's stomach.

Callie let go of the hose as the man fell to the ground, dropping his gun.

But as quickly as he fell, he recovered, and his arm snaked out for the revolver. Frank kicked at the gun but missed. He got the guy's hand instead. The man bellowed. The pain seemed to enrage him, and he hurled himself forward until his fingertips just touched the cold steel.

Frank took in the situation in a flash and grabbed Callie's hand. "Let's go!"

They raced to the van as the man's hand circled the butt of the gun and he staggered to his feet, ready to shoot.

Frank sped down Bay Road, quickly leaving the cottage far behind. Even though he kept his eyes straight ahead of him, he did notice a smile forming on Callie's face.

"You wanted to come on this *alone,* didn't you?" she said smugly.

"You did a good job," Frank admitted. "Although I did have a plan to deal with that guy."

"Oh, come on, Frank! Admit it, you'd have been sunk without me—"

Frank laughed. "All right, all right, I admit it! Now maybe you can help me figure out what was going on back there. The whole place was ransacked, but an expensive camera was left on a tripod upstairs, completely untouched."

"Was Simone a photographer?"

"Not that I know of. The only thing I can think is that the camera belonged to that gunman. But why would he bring it up there?"

"I have a question, too," Callie said. She pulled a long, colorfully patterned silk scarf out of her handbag. "Whose is this? I found it behind one of the armchairs."

Frank glanced at it quickly. "Somehow I don't think this belonged to our pistol-packing friend. I'd say it was Aunt Gertrude's, but it's a little too—too—"

"High fashion? I agree. Doesn't look like the kind of thing she'd wear."

"We'll have to ask her later," Frank said as he caught a glimpse of a small wooden sign.

VICTUALS AND GROG
IN AN OLD-TIME SETTING
* THE SHORE INN *
ENTERTAINMENT NIGHTLY

"Last stop," Frank said.

"Oh, good," Callie remarked with a smile. "I'm hungry."

"We can't stay—I promised Joe we'd be right back."

They pulled into a gravel driveway. At the end of it was an old red-brick building with smoke rising from the chimney. A brass plaque on the front wall said "The Shore Inn—1737. Here lodged the young Benjamin Franklin on his way to Philadelphia to seek his fortune."

Frank parked the van next to the only other three cars in the parking lot. As he and Callie got out, the loud thump of a song's bass line rattled the ground-floor windows.

"I wonder what Ben Franklin would have thought of *that*," Frank mused.

They walked through the front door and looked around. Dark wooden chairs rested upside down on top of round tables, and a long, shiny mahogany bar stretched along one wall. Right next to it, two enormous oak doors led into what must have been the kitchen. Frank heard chopping noises. The music echoed loudly through the building, and three workers boogied to it as they swept and cleaned up. One was muscular, running to fat. The second was taller, with a sprinkling of acne scars across his face. The third was tall and weedy—he was singing along with the record, using his broomstick as a microphone.

Just then a tall redheaded woman burst through the swinging oak doors. Her lips were drawn into a straight, tight line. "All right, guys. Knock it off!" she ordered. "We're trying to talk in here!"

The worker behind the bar yanked the cassette from the tape deck. "Sorry, Mrs. Simone," he said.

Without answering, the woman whirled around and headed back toward the kitchen.

"Uh, excuse me! Mrs. Simone?" Frank called out.

The woman turned around again. When she saw Frank, she gave him a bored, dismissive look. "We're not hiring anybody right now," she said, walking through the door. "Check back with me in the spring, okay?"

Frank rushed over to the door and held it open. "That's not why I'm here, Mrs. Simone," he replied. "I want to talk to you about your ex-husband!"

The woman turned around and eyed Frank suspiciously.

"You are Mrs. Henry Simone, aren't you?" Frank asked.

"Yes," she answered, her face drawn and tight. She followed Frank back into the restaurant and let the door swing closed behind them. "And who are you?"

"My name is Frank Hardy, ma'am," he said. He pulled a couple of chairs off the nearest table. "Here—have a seat."

"Well, thank you," Alexandra Simone said

dryly as she sat down. "I like being made to feel welcome in my own restaurant."

"I, uh—I have some disturbing news for you, Mrs. Simone," Frank said, sitting opposite her. Callie was standing beside the bar. "Mr. Simone is—" He leaned across the table and tried to speak as gently as possible. "Well, he was found dead this morning."

Mrs. Simone leaned back in her chair and skeptically raised an eyebrow. "What is this, some sort of joke?"

"I wish it were," Frank said. "The police tried to reach you. It seems—it seems he was murdered."

Mrs. Simone stared at him in silence, her eyes narrowing. "How terrible," she finally said. "I mean, we weren't exactly on speaking terms, but I wouldn't have wanted anything like this to happen. Now, who did you say you were?"

Somehow Frank had expected a little more emotion than this. "Frank Hardy. I'm working to find out—"

"*Aiieeeeeee!*" A scream pierced the air. Frank wheeled around. Glasses crashed to the floor as Callie flailed her arms against the bar. Around her neck was the thick, muscular arm of the man they had escaped from at Henry Simone's cottage!

Frank bolted from his chair, ready to get the gunman. The three workers remained motionless, dumbfounded, until Callie's attacker called out, "Don't just stand there! Get the other kid! The guy!"

The three men rushed Frank. The linebacker going to seed was nearest. He tackled Frank. And as he fell, Frank grabbed onto the leg of a table and gave it a shake, sending the chairs toppling onto his assailant.

"Arrrggh!" The man lost his grip on Frank as he raised his arms to shield himself from the heavy chairs. Frank rolled away just in time to see the guy with the scars come up ready to jump him.

Frank leapt toward him and grabbed his ankles. The man tumbled—straight into the wall. Frank sprang to his feet as he saw Callie being pulled into the kitchen. "Hang on, Callie!" he called out.

But as he was running toward her, the weedy worker blindsided him, swinging the broom into Frank's midsection.

Frank's "Oof!" resounded through the empty restaurant. He clutched his side and fell facedown onto the floor. Instantly the thin guy tossed the broom aside and pounced on top of him, pulling his arms behind his back.

Frank struggled to escape his grip, but he gave up. It was no use. He was aware of heavy breathing all around him—and he realized that the other men had come to help their friend.

"Now hold still—unless you think you can breathe inside this slop bucket!" the thin guy told him.

"Nice," Frank retorted. "What else do you do around here for thrills?"

"We'll show you!" came the fat guy's voice. All at once Frank was pulled to his feet and shoved toward the kitchen. He crashed into one of the massive wooden doors, and it swung open, revealing Callie and Mrs. Simone backed up against a work counter while the gunman from the cottage stood in front of them with his revolver.

"Glad to see that the three of you could handle the kid," the man said sarcastically. "I hope he wasn't too hard on you."

The three men grumbled as they walked back out the door. Frank leaned against a rack of shelves, next to Callie. The stark, gleaming white walls of the kitchen were in jarring contrast to the dark restaurant.

"Are you all right?" Frank whispered to Callie.

"Couldn't be better, considering I was just grabbed by a two-hundred-pound goon who likes to beat up girls half his size."

The mysterious man let out an angry little snort. Mrs. Simone looked at him nervously and grabbed onto the side of the countertop. Behind them, a gray-haired, potbellied chef was busy chopping meat with a cleaver.

"What's going on, Eric?" Mrs. Simone asked. "Who are these kids?"

"I found them snooping around in your ex-husband's cottage," the man replied. "They seem to know something."

Frank glanced up and down the shelves to his left: a container full of chopped lettuce, a few jars of dressing, and a bottle marked Cayenne Pepper—uncovered and nearly empty.

"Which one of you kids is going to talk first?" the man asked.

Frank looked at Callie and shrugged. Callie looked at her shoes. Slowly Frank inched his arm along the shelf behind them.

"Well, uh—" he began. "We saw this car in the drive—"

"And we knew it wasn't Simone's car," Callie added. By now Frank was closing his fingers firmly around the cayenne bottle.

"So, we decided . . ." Callie said, trailing off.

The man glowered at Callie, impatient for her to continue her explanation. Then his eyes caught the slight motion behind her. He shot a glance at Frank and lunged forward. "Hey, what are you—"

"Duck, Callie!" Frank shouted. In one quick motion he grabbed the jar and hurled the contents in the man's face.

The gunman screamed, his hands going for his

eyes. Then he began coughing as the cloud of pepper got into his lungs.

"Come on, let's beat it!" Frank began coughing as the pepper got to him too. He grabbed Callie's hand. Together they sped toward the door. Frank extended his arm to push it open, just as a serious spasm of coughing hit him.

As he bent he felt something like a sudden gust of wind pass beside him. Frank knew what it was. He dove to the floor, pulling Callie with him.

And as he looked up he saw a foot-long carving knife wedged firmly in the wooden door, a foot from where he had been standing.

"Frank, watch it!" Callie shrieked, jumping to her feet.

Frank spun around, and his face blanched. The potbellied chef who had been peacefully ignoring them to cut up vegetables was now approaching them with a meat cleaver!

Chapter

6

FOR A GUY who looked like a little old man, the chef was surprisingly agile. He leapt toward Callie, but as Frank scrambled to his feet, the man swung around in midjump to slash at him.

Callie dove behind a worktable, and Frank backpedaled toward the door. "Hey, watch it, pal," he said. "Keep waving that around, and you'll get a nick in it—or us!"

The chef's face broke out into a gap-toothed grin as he closed in on Frank.

"Tell him to stop!" Callie shouted.

"Eric, this has gone too far!" Mrs. Simone said.

But the gunman couldn't hear; he had his head in the sink, trying to wash off the pepper.

Frank inched toward the kitchen door, remembering the knife stuck in it. The last thing he wanted was to get into a knife fight with a maniacal chef, but there didn't seem to be any alternative. . . .

The leering chef continued to slash the air with the cleaver. Frank ducked each slash. Then, with a sudden lunge, he turned and grabbed for the knife.

But his hands closed on thin air as the door was swung wide open. Before Frank could stop himself, he collided with Bayport Police Chief Collig.

"Frank! What are you doing here?" He looked at the knife embedded in the door. "Is this yours?"

"No, it's *his*, Chief Collig!" Frank pointed to the chef, who was now standing still, scratching his head.

"I threw it so it'd miss the kid. Just wanted to scare him," the chef said, his head down as he stared at his toes.

Chief Collig pulled the knife out of the door and shook it at the old man. "These aren't toys, you know."

Just then he caught sight of Mrs. Simone handing a towel to the tall stranger with water now streaming down his face. "Will someone tell me what is going on? I came here to meet with you and walked into a brawl. What's the matter, Clifton, you and Frank didn't like the food?"

Eric Clifton's face showed a mixture of anger and bewilderment as he toweled himself off. "You mean to tell me you know this kid?" he said.

"Sure do. Frank Hardy, a young detective." Chief Collig raised an eyebrow at Frank. "You two are in the same line of work."

"What?" Frank began.

Chief Collig laughed. "He may not look it, sopping wet, but Eric Clifton is the head of Elite Eye, the hotshot detective agency in New York City." He winked at Frank. "Who knows? If you play your cards right, maybe Mr. Clifton will offer you a job."

It all became clear to Frank. Clifton and he were doing the same thing—investigating Simone's murder. He felt a huge load lifted from his shoulders.

For the first time Clifton's face broke into a smile. "And I thought I was getting old and slow. I was up against two young pros!"

Callie beamed with pride.

"Well, I wouldn't say that," Frank replied. "Maybe two eager amateurs." He grinned over at Callie. "Have you guys picked up any leads?"

"Well, my associate and I have been gathering information today, which seemingly points to a woman Simone had been seeing, someone named Gertrude"—he paused and gave Frank a suspicious look—"Hardy."

Frank nodded. "She's my aunt, and she'd have a hard time swatting at a moth," Frank said. "I'm in this to prove she couldn't do it."

"I hate to say it, but it'll be hard, Frank. Everything points to her."

"What about the guy who shot Simone's clerk last week in New York?" Frank asked. "I think this has to involve a bad business deal of Simone's."

Clifton frowned. "Well, there is another good possibility. A close friend of Simone's who was also his accountant—a man named Justin Spears. Lately he's been extremely hostile to Mrs. Simone. She hired me, by the way, to protect her, in case he got any ideas."

"Do those three guys in the dining room work for you?" Frank asked, putting it all together.

Clifton nodded. "Bruno, and the cook too. Simone's will still names Alexandra as his beneficiary, even though they were divorced. If Spears got rid of both of them, he's next in line to inherit all of Simone's holdings."

"Well, it looks like things are progressing," Chief Collig said with a smile. "I'll—uh, be heading back to the station house to begin my own investigation." With that he walked back through the kitchen doors.

"So, when do we visit this Spears?" Callie asked.

"Am I to assume that you two are joining forces with us?"

"You bet," Callie said, looking at Frank. "Right?"

Frank shook his head. "Not so fast, Callie. I have to talk to Joe about this. It may not—"

"No need to rush things," Clifton said. "Sleep on it." He reached into his inside jacket pocket. "Here's my card—a little soggy, thanks to you, but still legible. If you're interested, why don't you come into the city and visit me in our office tomorrow."

Frank glanced quickly at Callie to quiet her. They couldn't decide right then whether or not to accept Clifton's invitation.

"Well, we'll see. Let's go, Callie. Good to meet you," Frank said, halfway to the door. He stopped short just then and reached into his pocket. "Oops, I almost forgot," he said, pulling out the silk scarf that Callie had found. "I picked this up in the parking lot. Anybody know who it belongs to?"

"Oh, I thought I'd lost that!" Alexandra Simone exclaimed, her face brightening. "Thank you so much!"

Frank smiled in return. He'd found another suspect.

Callie followed Frank out into the parking lot. "Just as I thought," he said. "She may be in on it in some way!"

"Brilliant, Sherlock," Callie said. "I knew she killed him! Of course, I may not be qualified to judge. I'm only an eager amateur. . . ."

Frank smiled sheepishly. "Sorry about that, Callie. Anyway, I shouldn't jump to conclusions about her just because of the scarf. Maybe she visited the cottage before Simone's death and left it there."

"Maybe," Callie replied with a shrug. "But she's the one with the motive. I mean, who knows how much she'll stand to gain from that will!"

"Well, let's just hope part of it isn't Aunt Gertrude's money. We'd better hurry—I told Joe I'd be back quick."

As he drove back to the station house, Frank thought about Clifton's offer. A connection with Elite Eye would give them information on Simone's business they couldn't get anyplace else.

He thought about the scarf. He had lied about where they found it, but as a result Elite Eye would remain on the wrong track.

It was at that moment Frank decided to take up Eric Clifton's invitation.

Even on the stairs up to the front door of the station house, Frank and Callie could hear yelling from inside. The loudest voice was unmistakable—Joe's.

"Uh-oh," Frank said. "Let's get him out of here before he gets himself arrested."

They pushed inside the doors and saw Joe locked in an argument with Officer Riley at the front desk. "What do you mean, she can't go home tonight? Can't you tell what this is doing to her? She's completely destroyed—she's not even making sense when she talks! We're not talking about a hardened criminal, Officer Riley. We're talking about my aunt. You're acting as if she's a murderer!"

Officer Riley nodded solemnly. "I understand your concern, Joe, but this new evidence—"

Joe threw his hands in the air. "What new evidence? You haven't even shown it to me!"

Frank stepped up beside his brother. "Hold on! What's happening here?"

"Frank!" Joe exclaimed, his face red. He pointed an accusing finger at Officer Riley. "We're talking cruel and unusual punishment here! Officer Riley wants to detain Aunt Gertrude overnight!"

"I'm sorry, boys," Riley said. "Believe me, I know how you feel. But we have some new evidence that's very, very disturbing. I think you should talk to a lawyer."

"What are you saying? Where's my aunt?" Frank cut in.

"She's still in the squad room, but we're going to have to transfer her to a cell soon."

Frank rushed past Officer Riley, followed by

Joe and Callie. He pushed open the door to the squad room.

Beside Riley's desk, Aunt Gertrude was rocking slowly back and forth, staring teary-eyed at the floor. She seemed to have aged twenty years since Frank had left her.

"Aunt Gertrude?" Frank said softly.

Gertrude Hardy blinked as if snapping out of a dream. "Frank!" she said, her eyes lighting up. "Oh, I'm so glad to see you! I feel so—so utterly degraded! It's bad enough just to *think* of this horrible thing, let alone be accused of doing it! And now this—forcing me to stay! I can't take it, Frank. It's making me crazy. They're—they're treating me as if I were a common criminal. Maybe they'll listen if both of you talk to them!"

Frank gently put his hand on his aunt's shoulder. "We'll take care of it," he said.

"Don't you worry," Joe chimed in. "Just sit tight."

They stepped outside to see Officer Riley heading down the hallway toward them. He was holding an envelope in his hand.

"Officer Riley, please," Frank said as he, Callie, and Joe walked into the hallway to meet him. "Have a heart—"

Con Riley held up his hand to stop Frank. "Chief Collig says I can show you the evidence. I—I don't think you're going to like what you see."

He held out the envelope to Frank, who opened it and took out a series of photos.

"What is this?" Callie said as she and Joe looked over Frank's shoulder.

Frank turned the top one over. It was a blurry black and white photo of the fishing pier, obviously taken from a great distance and then blown up. It had been taken at night, so only things in pools of light from the streetlamps were visible.

He noticed the outline of the pier and the railing and part of the supply house.

And then, on the bottom left, he saw the silhouette of a couple—an older man whose gray hair shone in the artificial light and a woman who was walking next to him with her arms folded.

They fell silent and motionless. In one of the photos the people looked remarkably like Aunt Gertrude and Henry Simone.

He flipped the photos. The next showed the same scene, except the couple had moved from left to right. In the third photo they couldn't be seen at all—they seemed to have disappeared into the darkness between the streetlights.

But it was the last picture that made Frank's stomach knot up. The man was no longer in the photo.

And the woman was hurrying away from the pier—alone!

Chapter

7

FOR A LONG TIME the three of them just stared at the picture. No one knew what to say.

"Is something wrong?" Aunt Gertrude called from inside the office. She wandered out and looked around at the group. "What's going on? Have they already tried and sentenced me?"

Instinctively Frank put the photos out of sight.

"No, Aunt Gertrude, of course not," Joe spoke up.

"I heard Officer Riley—and he said he had something to show you," Aunt Gertrude said. "What is it?"

"Just some, uh, circumstantial evidence. But don't worry, it's probably inadmissible in court anyway." He glared as Frank opened his mouth. This wasn't the time to tell her about the photos.

"Oh, can't you boys talk to me in plain English?" Aunt Gertrude answered, her brow furrowed. She gave Frank a curious look. "And just what are you hiding?"

Frank looked at the ground sheepishly. "We're going to have to show her sometime, Joe," he said.

As Officer Riley watched solemnly, Frank handed the photos to Aunt Gertrude.

"You all look like you've just seen a ghost. What are these anyway?" She yanked them out of the envelope and flipped through them.

Frank watched as the color drained from Aunt Gertrude's face. "These people look like—like— Where did you get these?" she asked, her voice almost a whisper.

"They were sent to us anonymously," Officer Riley replied. "No note, just the pictures."

"And—and you think these people are Cyril and myself." Aunt Gertrude's eyes had become round with fear.

"Well, are they?" Officer Riley asked.

"Of course not!" Aunt Gertrude snapped. "We're not the only people who have taken walks at the pier at night. I don't understand how—" She swallowed hard and looked around her. "Oh! All of a sudden I'm not feeling well—" She dropped the photos on the floor.

Joe grabbed her arm. "Look how upset you've gotten her!" he said to Officer Riley.

"Let me take her to the rest room to pull herself together," Callie suggested.

Officer Riley looked from Callie to the Hardys. "All right," he said. "It's down the hall and to the left."

Callie reached for Aunt Gertrude's arm, but Aunt Gertrude put up her hands to stop her. "I—I can go by myself," she insisted.

She walked down the hall, her head high.

Officer Riley shrugged. "Sorry, folks."

Joe picked up the photos and said, "This is ridiculous. There's no evidence here at all! And besides, isn't it a little strange that someone would be sitting around snapping pictures of people at the pier in the dark?"

Con Riley shrugged his shoulders. "We're only at the beginning of this case."

"I know, but—"

At that moment a loud thud interrupted them from down the hall.

"What was that?" Frank said.

"Don't know. Came from the rest rooms," Officer Riley answered, running toward the noise. "I hope she's all right."

Before Officer Riley could finish his sentence, Frank, Joe, and Callie had raced ahead of him.

When they got to the women's room, Frank and Joe started to push through the door.

"Hey!" Callie yelled, stopping them.

Frank felt himself blush as he and Joe stood back so Callie could go in.

Through the closed door came rattling noises and the muffled sounds of Aunt Gertrude's and Callie's voices.

Before long the door opened. Callie had her arm around Aunt Gertrude, supporting her. The older woman looked as though she had been crying.

"It's all right," Callie said softly. "Let's just sit down."

Aunt Gertrude sobbed softly as she was led into the police lounge. "I—I just feel so trapped. Nobody's going to believe me!"

Callie helped her to lie down on a couch in the lounge.

"Squaaaawk! Can't whistle without my vittles!"

They both jumped at the parrot's screeching. Aunt Gertrude had forgotten that Con Riley had taken the bird to the station house for safekeeping.

As Callie glared at the bird, it said, "No sweat! Brrrock!" Callie glanced back at Aunt Gertrude, but she had leaned back and shut her eyes. She seemed calmer, so Callie went back out.

"What happened in there?" Frank asked.

Callie shot Officer Riley a confused but angry look. "She fell down."

"She what?" Riley said.

"She fell down!" Callie repeated fiercely.

Not until she and the Hardys were outside did she tell them what had really happened. "I went in and found her trying to escape out the window."

Frank and Joe stared at Callie, a tense silence falling over them. No one could say it, but it was clear that Aunt Gertrude was not acting like an innocent person.

"You can't see through these windows!" Joe complained, trying to get a view of the New York City skyline as the train trundled along the next morning. The boys luckily had the day off from school.

Frank shrugged his shoulders as he glanced at the badly scratched Plexiglas. "Oh, well, we paid them to get us there, not entertain us."

Foooosh! As if in answer to Joe's problem, the train plunged into a tunnel, and everything around them was pitch-black.

Joe sat back in his seat. "You sure Callie didn't stow away on this train? She might be in some disguise. You know, a thin, peach-faced man with a bushy mustache and a high-pitched voice—"

"Nope," Frank said with a laugh. "I had a long talk with her this morning. Besides, she knows that it wouldn't be proper at a funeral."

Clifton had called them the night before to tell them Simone was being buried that day. The boys hadn't the heart to tell their aunt—she had wanted to go to the funeral but was still being detained.

"Last stop, New York!" the conductor's voice rang out. "Remember to take all personal belongings!"

"Let's go!" Frank said, stepping into the crowd of people jamming the aisle to get out.

As Joe followed his brother out of the train, he self-consciously pulled down the legs of his dark suit, which were riding up his calves. "I can't figure out what happened to this thing. It fit me last spring."

"Growing pains," Frank replied.

When they got onto the platform, Frank led Joe through a warren of tunnels to the subway, which whisked them downtown.

They emerged four stops later in Greenwich Village, which always reminded Frank of a citified Bayport. Once they got away from the busy avenues, they walked down a quiet residential street of tightly packed brownstone buildings. The late-morning sunlight shining through the leaves of the small trees lining the block dappled the sidewalk. About halfway down the block, people were filing into a building with a small sign that said Moretti Brothers Funeral Home.

As they crossed the street to the funeral parlor, Frank and Joe noticed two men stop in front of the building. One was thin, dark, and balding, with a neatly tailored blue suit. He looked uncomfortable speaking to the other man, a broad-shouldered guy who strained the seams of an expensively tailored gray suit and chomped on a cigar as he listened.

A raised voice carried. "It's merely an accounting procedure, Norm," the balding man said. "I do it to adjust cash-flow figures, for tax purposes."

The other man pulled the cigar out of his mouth and waved it as he spoke. "I wasn't born yesterday, Spears. My assistants are going nuts over this!"

"Unbelievable," Joe said quietly because they were now ten feet from the men. "Talking about business, even at a funeral."

" 'Spears,' " Frank whispered. "That's the name that Clifton mentioned."

At that moment Clifton came out of the funeral parlor, a quizzical look on his face. "Ah, Frank and Joe!" he called out. "Good to see you." He stepped down the stairs, shook their hands, and glanced at the other two men. "Have you all met? Frank—and I assume this is Joe Hardy." Joe nodded. "This is Justin Spears, Mr. Simone's accountant, and Norman Fleckman, one of his close business associates. Frank and Joe are helping me on this case."

Frank was surprised that Clifton would be so open about it, but Clifton gave him a reassuring look. "These two men have agreed to provide information on Simone and his activities."

"How do you do?" Spears said, extending his hand.

Fleckman grunted and made his way up the stairs to the funeral parlor.

"We just got news that the priest has been delayed in traffic," Clifton said. "There's the big ticker-tape parade downtown for the World Series champs."

Spears looked at his watch and grimaced. "You know, it's a busy day for me. I'm afraid I'll have to be going after I offer my condolences to Mrs. Simone. By the way, I have something to show you, Eric."

"Well, I've really got to stick around. My first obligation is to Mrs. Simone. She's very upset. Frank and Joe, why don't you go with Mr. Spears to see what he has?"

"Of course," Frank said, looking curiously at Clifton.

As the accountant went in, Clifton held the Hardys back. "I thought you'd like to follow up on him, because if he's guilty, your aunt goes free," he explained. "Also, if he *is* hiding anything, he may let his guard down with a couple of kids."

Minutes later the three emerged from the funeral home. Spears led the way to the nearest avenue and hailed a cab to take them all downtown. Soon the low, stately brownstones gave way to Wall Street's huge glass and steel skyscrapers.

"This whole thing is baffling to me," Spears admitted as they sped down the street. He smiled modestly and adjusted his glasses. "My business is usually so—undramatic, you see. I just push numbers around. But now I've discovered some very suspicious things in my records."

The cab stopped in front of a thirty-story building with a set of brass-trimmed revolving doors. After Spears paid the cab driver, they all walked into a gleaming marble-walled lobby. Within seconds an elevator brought them to Spears's fifteenth-floor office. There was no secretary in the reception area.

"I hope my assistant hasn't gone out to lunch yet," Spears said. He turned the large brass knob and pushed against the polished mahogany door, which swung open. "Ah, good. He must be here. Enter, my friends."

But as Frank and Joe stepped into the room, they froze. Spears was right about his assistant being there—but he wasn't going to be of much use. He was sprawled unconscious on the floor on a bed of papers!

Spears's eyes widened as he took in the wreckage—drawers had been pulled out of filing cabinets, shelves were ripped out of the walls, his desk was overturned. This hadn't been a search. Someone had simply trashed the office.

Spears gasped when he looked up and saw the wall above his desk. In thick, bold letters, the word *beware* had been scrawled in blood!

Chapter

8

JOE KNELT BESIDE the assistant, who was curled up next to a filing cabinet, his blond hair across his face. There didn't seem to be any cuts or bruises. Joe felt the young man's wrist. "He's got a pulse," he said, then gently shook the man.

"Wha-what's going on?" The assistant's eyes flickered open, and he jerked himself away from Joe. "Get your hands off me! I swear I'll call the police!"

"Easy, easy," Joe replied softly. "We're here to help. Mr. Spears is with us."

"Justin?" the man answered, still dazed. A look of relief washed over his face as he saw his boss.

"Are you okay, Bart?" Spears asked, and the man nodded. "What happened here?"

71

Bart's look of relief disappeared as he sat up and looked around the office. He put his hand to his forehead, obviously in pain, remembering what had happened.

"I—I don't know," he said. "There was a knock on the outer door, and it was two guys who said they were here to do the annual service on the copier. I let them in, and all of a sudden one of them came after me. So I backed away. . . ." He looked at the filing cabinet behind him and rubbed the back of his head. "I must have fallen against that."

As Joe helped Bart into a chair, Spears moved up close to inspect the wall that had been splattered with the word *beware*. "Some kind of red paint," he said, looking at the foot-high letters. "Someone is trying to scare me."

"Any idea who?" Frank asked.

Spears sank into the seat by his desk. "Well, no! I'm an accountant, not a—a boss of the underworld."

"You don't have any enemies? Anyone you've had a fight with?" Frank pressed.

"Wait a second!" Joe interjected. "What about that guy who was arguing with you outside the funeral home? What was his name again—Fleckman?"

Spears thought for a minute. "Norman Fleckman . . ." he said, nodding his head. "He's a client of mine. I do his financial records. Actually, we haven't been on good terms lately."

"Bad enough for him to do this to you?"

Spears sighed. "Well, I'm really not supposed to reveal client information—"

"This could be a clue in a murder case, Mr. Spears," Joe prodded. "We're up against a wall, and an innocent person has become the prime suspect."

Frowning, Spears considered Joe's words. Finally he answered. "Well, I suppose under the circumstances . . ." He shrugged once. "I may as well admit to you that I think Fleckman's business dealings are not always—shall we say, the most honest. He used to work with Simone at Thompson Welles, but then he branched off to form his own investment firm when some of the partners began complaining about his tactics." Spears gave a smile. "Simone could be very persuasive in his own quiet way, but Fleckman is much more—aggressive. In fact, so aggressive that he began stealing away some of Simone's clients.

"I can't prove it, but I think Fleckman got involved in a little bit of swindling. It seems, from what I've pieced together, that he'd carefully select his victims from among his elderly clients, people who didn't know the market, who depended on him to explain everything to them. He'd tell them their stocks had tumbled—that their money was as good as gone. Get their signature on a paper. But in reality the stocks had actually doubled or tripled. That's how I think it worked, but I can't prove it—yet.''

"I can see what Simone had against Fleckman, but what did Fleckman have against him?" Frank asked.

"The more clients Simone lost, the angrier he got. So he started to put together bits of information about Fleckman and his shady dealings. I think he threatened to blow the whistle on him.''

"Something bothers me about this," Frank said. "Simone's record had to have been pretty spotless if he was willing to expose Fleckman.''

"That's right," Spears said. "Henry Simone was completely honest.''

"Then why the alias?" Joe asked. "And what did he do with our aunt Gertrude's money?''

Spears looked blank. "I don't know. He might have taken an alias to escape Fleckman. Maybe he was beginning to play rough. As for the money . . .''

"Maybe we should examine Simone's records," Frank suggested. "I'd like to see just *how* honest he was.''

Behind them, Bart had been fiddling with the computer terminal, trying to see if it was still working.

"Bart, call up Simone's file, will you please?" Spears asked.

Bart's fingers danced over the keyboard. Instantly the screen showed columns and columns of numbers with the name SIMONE, HENRY above them.

The four of them sat around the screen as Spears explained the numbers. Every cent was accounted for.

Spears pressed a few keys and a new set of figures appeared on the screen, with the heading PERSONAL INCOME AND INVESTMENTS. "Unfortunately," Spears explained, "Mr. Simone made a few bad investments for himself and died with very little money of his own."

Frank and Joe examined the screen. Sure enough, many of Simone's investments showed losses, and his net worth was very little.

Frank noticed there was no reference to his aunt Gertrude's money going into Simone's account. Where was it? And how could he tell her that her life savings had disappeared?

"So his ex-wife wouldn't have done him in for his money?" Joe said.

Spears laughed. "If so, she'd be in for a big surprise."

So much for Clifton's suspicion about Spears as the next beneficiary, Frank thought. "If you don't mind, Mr. Spears, I'd like a copy of Simone's and Fleckman's records. I'll be discreet and give them back soon. I have a feeling this case is going in a new direction."

"It's highly irregular, but if you promise to keep them confidential," Spears answered. "Bart, will you please print out a copy?"

As Frank and Joe left the office with the evidence, they heard the solid click of the office door's deadbolt.

"Okay, next stop, Elite Eye," Frank said. "I'd like to point out a new suspect to Eric Clifton."

Joe laughed and glanced through the records as they walked toward the elevator. "Look at this!" he said. "Half of Simone's client accounts were closed out this past week!"

As Frank reached for the papers, he heard a distant *ding*.

"Come on!" he said. Running around the corner toward the elevator, he shouted, "Hold the door, please!"

At the end of the long cream-colored hallway, two men in suits were leaning against a wall across from the elevator doors. As the doors started to shut, one of them reached out to hold them open.

Frank and Joe ran into the elevator. "Hey, just in the nick of time," Frank said. "Glad you guys were standing there."

Frank had assumed the two men would stay on the floor, since they hadn't gotten into the elevator when the doors had first opened. But instead, they walked into the elevator. "We're going down too," one of them said in a cold voice.

The man pressed M for the main floor and stood against the back of the elevator. His husky friend eyed Frank and Joe silently, one hand in his pocket. The elevator motor hummed as they descended.

Frank wasn't sure, but he thought he saw the men share an almost imperceptible glance.

The lights above the elevator door flicked on and off at each floor: 9, 8, 7 . . .

Suddenly on six Frank reached out and pressed the number 5 on the panel. "Oops," he said. "Almost forgot to press our floor!"

"What are you—" Joe began, but Frank shot him a silencing glance.

The door whooshed open on the fifth floor, and Frank stepped out, pulling Joe with him. As Frank set a fast pace down the hallway, they heard the sound of the elevator closing behind them.

"What was that all about?" Joe demanded.

"Shhh!" Frank whispered. "Just look for the stairs!"

Joe wasn't sure what Frank was getting at, but he knew better than to doubt his brother's judgment when it came to quick thinking. He turned around, looking for an exit sign, and immediately saw that they weren't the only ones in the hallway.

Behind them, racing forward, were the two men from the elevator.

A few steps ahead of Joe, Frank rounded a corner. "Here it is!" he shouted.

The brothers shot through the door marked Exit A and scuttled down the cement stairs. The *chunk-chunk-chunk* of their footsteps was answered by heavier footsteps above them. Taking two steps at a time, Frank and Joe raced past the fourth-, third-, and second-floor landings. From the second floor to the ground level was a stairway, flanked by a smooth metal banister, twice as long as the others. Below them was the door to the lobby.

"There's only one way to do this," said Joe, hiking himself up onto the banister.

"Go for it!" Frank replied. "I'll hop on after you!"

With a loud whoop the Hardy brothers slid down to the first floor. When they got to the bottom, Joe hopped off and rammed his shoulder against the metal exit door.

Whomp! The sound of the impact echoed through the stairwell.

Joe grunted in pain and staggered back. He tried to push again, but the door wouldn't budge. "What's going on here?"

He stood back from the door to examine it. "Uh-oh," Frank muttered.

In the dim light they could read a large metal sign that was screwed into the door. Its red letters said No Re-entry on This Floor. Go to 2.

A new sound—that of clomping feet—grew loud behind them. They were trapped.

Chapter

9

FRANK AND JOE swung around and looked up. The bare light bulb on the second-floor landing created two broad silhouettes as the two men ran down the stairs.

Joe tensed his body and looked at his brother. "Ready?" he asked.

"Yeah, let's go for it!"

Together, Frank and Joe leapt up at the men's legs.

"Hey, wait!" one of them cried out. He tried to climb back up the stairs, but it was too late. Joe's arms locked around his knees, and the two of them tumbled to the ground-floor landing.

"Stop!" the man said as Joe pinned him to the ground in a wrestling hold.

With a muted *whomp*, Frank and the other man

landed on the floor next to them. "What are you guys doing?" Frank's adversary protested. "We didn't do anything to you!"

Joe's fist was poised in the air. "That's right," the man beneath him said. "And don't think we couldn't mess you up if we wanted to!"

"Who are you?" Joe demanded.

"We work for Norman Fleckman," the man said. "He told us to find you and bring you to his office. Peacefully."

Joe was baffled. "How did he know we were here?"

"And why didn't you tell us about yourselves before?" Frank added.

"He overheard you saying you'd go to Spears's office," came the answer. "So we came up and staked out the elevator."

Frank and Joe got up and brushed themselves off. "What do you think, Frank?" Joe asked.

"I think we should meet this Fleckman character," Frank answered, picking up the envelope of financial records. He turned back to the two men. "All right, guys, take us to your leader."

Joe exhaled loudly, pacing back and forth on the cool gray carpet of the reception area. He and Frank had just discovered a suspect to get the police investigation moving in a new direction— and get their aunt Gertrude out of jail. But they were stuck in a high-rise tomb, waiting.

From behind a long desk a young man looked up and said, "Mr. Fleckman should be out any minute now. It's been a long morning."

Joe just grunted and continued pacing.

Suddenly a gruff voice sounded over the intercom on the desk. "Albert, I want the Sullivan file right away. Send a memo to Skinner: sell! Get Norita on the phone in Tokyo, tell him the real-estate deal is off, and get me a turkey club and black coffee. Got it?"

"Yes, sir," the secretary said, rolling his eyes.

"Late lunch?" Joe asked.

The secretary shrugged. "One-thirty isn't so late."

The intercom cracked again. "Oh, and send those kids in here, will you?"

"There you have it," the young man said dryly. "His highness has spoken. First door on your left."

Frank and Joe walked into Fleckman's office. Stacks and stacks of papers lay all over the shelves, the floor, the chairs. A phone in one hand and a cigar in the other, Norman Fleckman sat at a desk by the window.

This place looks almost as bad as Spears's did, Joe thought. And nobody's even ransacked it.

"What do you mean, pork bellies have bottomed out?" Fleckman shouted into the phone. "You're just trying to dump your bad holdings on me. Nah! Nah, get outta here, Seymour. I don't want to talk to you!''

With a loud crash he slammed the phone down. "Love that guy, he's a barrel of laughs," he muttered. Then he pressed a button and said, "Albert, no calls."

Swiveling in his chair, he looked up at Frank and Joe and held out a large brass box. "Cigars?" he offered with a wide, toothy grin.

"Uh, no thanks," Joe answered.

"Good boy," Fleckman said, retracting the box. "They'll kill you. Have a seat." He pointed to two overstuffed chairs across from his desk. "Don't mind the mess."

Frank and Joe each sat on the edge of a chair, the only spots in the room that weren't completely covered with papers.

"We ran into two of your men—" Joe began.

Fleckman waved his hand dismissively. "Hope those goons weren't any trouble to you. Anyway, I wanted you boys here because I want to make you a deal. Anyone helping Eric Clifton in this case is a friend of mine. By the way, sad about Simone, isn't it? Fine man."

"Some people thought so," said Joe.

Fleckman raised an eyebrow and gave Joe a piercing glance. "Yes," he said, letting a cautious silence sit in the air for a few seconds. Then he leaned forward, uncovered an ashtray, and stubbed out his cigar. "Let me ask you guys a

83

question. I saw you leaving with Spears. Now, what exactly did he tell you?''

"Is that why you sent your stooges to abduct us?" Joe snapped. "To grill us about something that isn't your business?"

"I see we're not going to have fun with this." Fleckman sighed. He leaned over his desk, his eyes shifting from Frank to Joe and back. "Okay, I know Spears must have talked, and I'm sure he gave you the old this-is-between-me-and-you line and I-don't-have-any-proof-but. . . . Told you I was a swindler, right? I took Simone's clients, blah, blah, blah—''

"Maybe. Maybe not," Joe replied. "Why? Do you have a different story?"

"Let me tell you something, kid." Fleckman leaned across his desk. "You don't get to where I am by playing it totally clean. But I'm a nice guy compared to Henry Simone. If you want to know about swindling, good old Henry wrote the book. It's common knowledge in the industry that he came up with the most creative scams. In fact, most of my clients came to me because they felt they'd lost their shirts with Simone.''

"You have any proof to back that up?" Frank asked.

"I'll bet Spears showed you records on a computer screen, right? That's because he can change the figures easily. If he wants to show that Simone was clean''—he tapped his fingers on the desk as if he were typing—"*click, click, click*, he presses a few buttons and the records of scams disappear out of Simone's account." His eyes flared with anger. "And into mine! The guy's setting me up to look like a crook while he keeps all the illegal money!"

"I see," Frank said. "And I suppose you can tell us why Spears would do this to you?"

"I began suspecting that something was up, and my computer consultant was able to confirm that Spears was tapping into his accounting records." He rose from his chair and began pacing. "But I still can't figure *why*. Has he been paid off to protect Simone's reputation? Does he have a grudge against me? I just don't know."

"Seems to me you could just fire him," Frank said.

Fleckman sat at the edge of his desk. "Very smart—you're good. I'll fire him all right, but first I've got to clean my record, or I'll end up having to explain all this phantom money."

"And you expect us to help," Frank said matter-of-factly.

"I need someone who knows Spears, someone who can keep an eye on him, someone he has no reason to distrust. And you can be sure there'll be ample reward for this. Now, I know a couple of snappy young fellows like you can use a hot new car, some jazzy clothes—" He reached into his desk drawer and took out a leather-bound checkbook. "Just name your price—or should I say, consultants' fee!"

Frank stood up. "Sorry, Mr. Fleckman. We want to search out the truth as much as you do, but we're not working for anyone. We want only to clear our aunt."

As the brothers walked toward the door, Fleckman followed them. "You're honorable guys," he said, opening the door for them. "I like that. I respect it. Just remember, my offer will be there if you change your minds."

"We won't," Frank said. With that, he and Joe walked through the reception area and into the hallway.

Behind them, they could hear Fleckman shouting, "I said a turkey club, Albert! Not a hero!"

As they walked along, Joe said under his breath, "I guess he's used to people doing whatever he wants."

"From getting his lunch to trashing someone's office," Frank added. "I don't know if I trust him." They reached the elevator bank and pressed the Down button.

"I don't know if I trust him or Spears. Both stories have lots of holes. How could Simone have been broke and able to live in semiretirement in Bayport? And if Fleckman's records were really sabotaged, why didn't he just hire someone to audit his records and show what Spears was doing to him?"

"Down!" a voice called out as an elevator door lurched open.

"Ground floor, please," Frank told the uniformed operator, who shut the door.

Bzzzzzt. On the elevator-control panel the light for the third floor flicked on. Joe glanced at it and noticed that the operator passed right by the floor.

"Aren't you supposed to stop?" Joe asked.

The man played with the controls, but nothing happened. "Must be broken—" he mumbled.

Joe looked at Frank. Suddenly he felt very uneasy. They counted off the floors on the indicator light. It flashed to 2, then M.

And then B, for basement. And then SB, for subbasement . . .

"Hey, where are you taking us?" Joe demanded.

Now the man was fiddling energetically with the controls. "Dumb thing won't stop!"

"I don't believe this," Joe whispered to his brother. "Kidnapped by an elevator!"

The elevator kept dropping, finally stopping on SB3, three levels below the ground. As the door slid open, Frank and Joe stepped out to look around. They were in a long, dark concrete-block hallway. Behind them they heard the final click as the elevator door slid closed.

"Sorry, fellas, this elevator is out of service,"

the operator said. The boys could hear the chuckle in his voice.

"Thanks a lot," said Frank. "It was a pleasure flying with you."

With that, Frank and Joe stalked down the hall in search of a flight of stairs.

Instead, they saw the two men who'd brought them to Fleckman, flanked by two huge men in custodial uniforms.

Thinking fast, Joe said to the men, "There you are! The elevator is stuck down here, guys. Do you think you can fix—"

The men began to approach them silently. The brothers backed away.

"Okay, uh, why don't we run back and wait for you?" Frank and Joe spun around and bolted down the hallway.

The four men filled the corridor in back of them. In front of them the hallway ended at a door that appeared to be locked.

"You've got no choice, boys," the goon with the cold voice said. "And unfortunately, neither do we. Come on."

The men surrounded Frank and Joe, unlocked the door, and led them through dimly lit corridors that wound through the subbasement. Before long they heard a loud grinding noise.

The Hardys looked at each other. "What's that?" Joe asked.

"You'll see soon enough," the leader of the

men said. "The boss said to dispose of you. So—"

They'd reached the end of the hallway. Now Frank and Joe could make out the words on the door.

The sign said Trash Compactor.

Chapter
10

A SICKENING METALLIC shriek pierced the air as the man pushed the door open. Frank and Joe looked inside the cramped, dingy room. The walls, which had once been painted white, were now encrusted with cobwebs and dirt. Sour-smelling bags of trash were piled several feet high on the floor.

And in the middle of the room, an ironclad black machine stretched from the floor to the ceiling, vibrating wildly and letting out an ear-splitting noise.

"There's your compactor," one of the men answered, hiking up his dark green uniform pants around his overhanging belly. "It's in the middle of a load."

"What fool turned it on?" the leader barked.

"I did," the potbellied man said. "You know, Fleckman called only five minutes ago, and I wanted to get a load of trash in before—"

THWOOMP! CRRRUNCH! As the noise echoed through the room, Joe felt sick to his stomach.

"You know we can't stop that thing, or put anything in it, once it starts? Where were you when they handed out brains?"

"W-well, it's coming to the end of the cycle," the custodian said defensively.

Slowly the noise began to subside.

"I guess we're stopping here to check out the trash on the way upstairs, huh, guys?" Joe asked.

"We're going upstairs all right," the other maintenance man said with a toothless grin. "But you'll be coming out a lot shorter."

At that moment the great machine stopped. The leader opened a door in the front of it, releasing an even fouler odor into the room. He pulled out a grotesque three-foot-wide object—a dense, battered-looking combination of paper, folders, metal brackets, and food wrappers, all crushed into a neat little cube.

Joe swallowed hard. Out of the corner of his eye he could see his brother staring poker-faced at the machine. Joe knew that look. It meant Frank was baffled and was feverishly trying to come up with a plan.

"All right," the leader said, shifting his eyes from man to man. "Throw 'em in."

Brawny arms grabbed Frank and Joe, jerking them toward the open door.

"J-just a minute!" Frank shouted at the top of his lungs. "We've got something Fleckman ought to see!"

"What are you talking about?" the cold-voiced goon demanded.

"We got papers from Spears—the guy who's trying to foul Fleckman up." Frank was almost babbling as he spread out Spears's printouts on top of a panel connected to the trash compactor by a wire.

Joe stared at his brother, wide-eyed. Had he gone berserk? Had he truly given up?

But as he watched Frank spread the printouts with his right hand, he noticed Frank's left hand creeping over to a small switch on the panel.

The leader, who had been trying to make sense of the accounting gobbledygook, turned back to Frank and said, "Just tell me what this proves and I'll—" His eyes popped wide open. "Hey, what are you doing?"

Frank lunged and flicked the switch. With a loud *chunk!* the compactor's door slammed shut.

A deep humming sound filled the room as the machine started up—with nothing to compact.

"You rotten—" The leader, followed by the largest of Fleckman's goons, rushed Frank.

Joe wasted no time. In the confusion he spun around and flicked off the light switch, plunging the room into total darkness. Loud crashes and shouts of pain resounded as Frank and the others tripped over the trash on the floor.

And in the midst of it all, a high-pitched whistle pierced the air.

Frank, letting me know where he is, Joe thought. He groped around and found the door and knob. Then, as loud as he could, he let out a whistle of his own.

In the darkness he heard low stumbling noises.

"Yeeouch!" came a low, unfamiliar voice.

"Oof!" came another. A third yell was followed immediately by a fourth.

"I'm coming, Joe!" Frank's voice called out. In seconds Frank stumbled against his brother, and they both pushed their way through the door.

As they slammed it behind them, another frustrated yell sounded from inside.

"I got all four of them," Frank said. "Let's get out of here before one of them gets up."

Pushing at top speed, they followed the cinderblock hallway to a stairwell. Flinging the door open, they hauled themselves up three flights of dingy stairs until, panting, they stumbled into the building lobby and out the door.

The honking of horns and the roar of traffic was a welcome sound to their ears as they ran out to the crowded street.

"How do we get to Elite Eye?" Joe shouted to Frank, close on his heels.

"I'm not sure! Let's find a phone and call!" Frank answered.

At the end of the block was a bank of four outdoor pay phones. One of them was empty, and Joe grabbed it. He shoved a quarter into the slot and dialed Clifton's number.

"I'm sorry, your call requires a twenty-five-cent deposit," a recorded voice droned.

"But I *did* deposit—" Joe began to shout. Then he saw the person next to him hang up and walk away from her phone. He reached over and lifted the receiver—and felt a huge hand on his shoulder.

"Hey, pal, I was on line here!" the guy connected to the hand complained.

Joe turned all the way around to see a group of harried people waiting for the phones. All were glowering angrily at him—especially the man-mountain who had been first.

"Never mind, Joe! Follow me!" Frank shouted. He had just spotted a Chinese restaurant and knew a phone would be inside. They rushed inside and Joe once again dialed Clifton.

"Friendly place, this city—" he said under his breath. "Hello, Joe Hardy for Eric Clifton, please!"

Immediately he heard, "Yes, Joe, where are you?"

Joe craned his neck to see the street sign outside. "Rector and Greenwich, down in the financial district. Are we near you?"

"No. What are you doing down there?"

"We had a run-in with Fleckman. He knew we were talking to Spears, and—"

"Fleckman! Who told you to— I should have warned you. Stay clear of that guy. He's ruthless—especially if he needs something from you."

"Now you tell me," Joe muttered.

"What's that?"

"Never mind. Listen, we've got more suspects than we know what to do with. Fleckman tried to kill us, Spears may have lied to us. And you'd better know, we found Alexandra Simone's scarf at Simone's cottage—"

"What? Alexandra—hmm, you know, I've been having suspicions about her. Listen. Meet me in half an hour at the train station at the gate for Bayport. I think it's time we confronted Mrs. Simone—and on the way there you can tell me about your other evidence. Get a move on and stay away from Fleckman."

"Right!" Joe slammed down the phone and said, "Follow me, Frank!"

Without wasting a moment they barged out of the restaurant. "Okay," Joe said, looking around. "Wall Street . . ." He noticed a crowd of people at a nearby bus stop and asked one of them, "Excuse me, where's the Wall Street subway?"

He didn't answer Joe. An elderly tourist couple said, "We'll let you use our guidebook if you'll point us toward the World Trade Center."

While Frank pointed the way, Joe flipped through the downtown street maps. "It's just up this street and a couple of blocks—"

He looked around—to find himself staring up into the surprised eyes of one of Fleckman's goons. "Thanks!" He handed the tourists their guidebook, then he and Frank raced uphill along the street.

When they got to the top, they turned a corner to find a crowd filling the street shoulder to shoulder. Hundreds of backs were moving as people craned their necks, trying to watch something the Hardys couldn't see.

Frank and Joe started back down the hill, but stopped when they noticed all four of Fleckman's goons rushing them. There was only one way to go.

"Excuse me—excuse me—" Frank and Joe said, pushing their way through the crowd.

People called out as the Hardys pressed desperately onward: "Hey, knock it off!" "Don't push me, man!" "Where are you going, pal? This is a parade!"

Sure enough, Joe glanced up to see a motorcade rolling down the street. In front of it was a large banner that said NYC WELCOMES ITS OWN WORLD SERIES CHAMPS! Ticker-tape and computer paper rained down from the skies.

"I wonder how much of this will end up in a trash compactor," Frank mused, elbowing people right and left.

In convertible limos baseball players sat waving triumphantly to the crowd. Between the cars walked more of the players, bat boys, front-office people, and others. Everyone was whooping it up. "I don't even recognize half those people!" said Joe. "Maybe we could fit in with them!"

They burst through the crowd and vaulted over the police barricade that lined the street. "Now, look triumphant!" Joe said as they joined the parade. They marched with a group of celebrating ballplayers, waving and throwing kisses into the crowd.

The four men had reached the barricade by now, and the potbellied goon ducked under first. He was met on the other side by a large, annoyed policeman, tapping a billy club into his palm.

After a few blocks Frank and Joe scanned the onlookers and saw no sign of their attackers.

"Let's get out of here!" Joe said.

The two brothers slipped away from the parade and back into the crowd, where they finally made their way toward the subway.

* * *

"All aboard the Bridgefield train, leaving Track Eighteen in one minute!" the voice echoed through the train station.

"Come on!" Joe called to his brother. "That's the one that stops in Bayport! We've got to get aboard!"

Frank and Joe hurried to the top of the stairs. The station was especially jammed with people who had come to town for the parade. Below them, a throng of people was scrambling to get into the train before the doors closed. Joe caught a glimpse of Eric Clifton boarding one of the cars.

"Clifton's in the second car up!" Joe called back to Frank. The two of them tried to make some headway in that direction.

"Welcome to New York," Joe muttered. "It feels like all I've done today is fight crowds."

"That may not be all we'll have to fight," Frank said in his ear. "Look who's over there."

Joe glanced to his right and fell silent. Forcing their way down the stairs and onto the platform were two familiar faces—the goons Fleckman had sent. They were without the custodians this time though; they must have split up. In the crush of the crowd, the jacket one of the thugs wore flapped open—revealing a leather shoulder holster!

The man pulled his jacket closed and stepped onto the train. In seconds another man squeezed *out* of the train.

"That was Bart, Spears's assistant!" Frank said.

"What's going on here?" Joe asked. He and Frank maneuvered their way halfway down the stairs to get closer to the train. They could just see Clifton sitting right beside the window. They also saw the two goons take seats—right behind him!

"Clifton!" Joe shouted as he tried to shove his way down to the train.

The doors closed tight just as Frank and Joe hit the platform.

"Fleckman knows who Clifton is and what he's investigating," said Frank. "He's probably got *those* guys after him too!"

"Clifton!" Frank and Joe shouted, running beside the train as it slowly started up. They pointed wildly to the seat behind him.

But as the train picked up speed and pulled away, Clifton just stared back at them, looking bewildered. Only Frank and Joe knew that behind him sat two armed killers.

Chapter

11

WITH A RHYTHMIC *chunk-a-chunk-a-chunk,* the brushed-chrome commuter train disappeared into the tunnel.

"What do we do now?" Joe asked.

His question was answered by the track announcer's next words:

"Three-thirty train for Kirkland now boarding. Track Twelve. All aboard!"

"Come on, Joe!" Frank said. "Kirkland's close to Bayport. We can catch a lift from there."

They ran back up the stairs and followed the crowd to Track 12. This time they were early for the train and grabbed two seats in a rear car.

As the train pulled out of the station, Frank looked out the window and drummed his fingers on his armrest. "I hope we're not too late," he said. Worry showed in his eyes.

Joe nodded. "I can just see the headlines: 'Commuter Shooter: Murder on the Bridgefield Express.' "

"They'll probably wait to nail Clifton until after they reach Bayport," Frank stated objectively.

"Sure, go ahead and be logical," Joe retorted.

The brothers fell into a gloomy silence as the train chugged through the tunnel. Their aunt Gertrude had spent the night and most of that day in jail, and the man who could help them get her out was riding on a train into a deathtrap.

"Thanks, Chet." Frank patted their friend Chet Morton on the shoulder as his car pulled up beside the Hardy van at the Bayport train station. Joe was already halfway out the door. "Call you later with the whole story."

As Frank climbed into the van's passenger seat, Joe was already shifting into first.

The van sped out onto the highway that ran beside the train tracks. "At least nothing happened at the station," Joe said as they ate up the road. In a few minutes they passed a sign that said Entering Cliffside Heights. Joe turned off the highway and drove through lazy, winding side streets. The houses here were larger and farther apart than the ones in the rest of Bayport, and each lawn seemed to be tended by a professional gardener.

"Do you remember the address Officer Riley mentioned for Mrs. Simone?" Joe asked. "Wasn't it Archer Street?"

Frank thought back. "Yeah. Four seventy-seven."

Joe turned onto Archer Street, while Frank looked out the window at the house numbers. "Hey, slow down!" Frank said. "There it is!"

Joe pulled the van in front of a large white colonial with a bay window. A manicured lawn sloped up to it, and a gravel driveway cut beside it to a three-car garage in back.

"Whew, a family could live in that garage," Joe remarked. "Alexandra Simone must be doing well."

Frank raced to the front door and pounded on it. "Mrs. Simone!" he called out. "It's Frank and Joe Hardy!"

Joe was still coming up the drive as the door was swung open by Alexandra Simone. "What's all this commotion, guys? I have a doorbell," she said.

"Look, we're sorry, but have you heard from Clifton? We lost him at the—"

"*You* lost *me?*" a voice behind Mrs. Simone said. "I'm the one who made the train!"

Frank's face brightened. "You made it! We thought that—"

Clifton nodded. "I picked up your hand gestures just fine. Besides, I'd had my eye on those two drones when they got on the train."

"What did you do? They were armed!"

"No kidding. The stop before Bayport, I got up and headed between the cars. When they followed me, I got the drop on them, took their guns, and locked them in one of the rest rooms." He grinned. "I even put a sign on it—Out of Order. They'll probably be in Bridgefield before they get loose. And I called the cops to meet them there."

Frank smiled. "Very neat."

At that moment they were interrupted by the sudden ringing of the phone.

"I'll get it," Mrs. Simone said, running into the kitchen.

Frank watched her leave and then turned to Clifton. "Did you tell her about the scarf?" he asked.

Clifton shook his head. "No, but I'm about to."

"Good, because we really should get back to the station house. Our poor aunt is probably going out of her mind."

"Clifton, it's for you!" came Mrs. Simone's voice from the kitchen. "It's urgent."

"Look, you go and take care of your aunt. I'll handle this end of it." He gave the brothers a wink before he started off to the kitchen. "Call me later."

Frank and Joe ran off to the van. "He's a good guy," Joe remarked as they climbed in.

"Sounds like he handled those goons pretty well," Frank agreed.

As they approached the station house, Joe gazed curiously into the parking lot. "That looks exactly like Dad and Mom's car," he said.

Frank looked over and caught a glimpse of the license plate. "That *is* their car. I guess they cut their trip short."

As soon as Joe parked the van, he and Frank darted into the station house. The first thing they heard was a calm but commanding voice.

"Chief Collig, I had to interrupt a perfectly wonderful and long-overdue vacation to come here. My sister sounded absolutely distraught over the phone. And my lawyer tells me you're detaining her on the absurd belief that she committed—"

Frank and Joe instantly recognized who it was. "Hey, Dad, welcome home!" Frank called out.

"I'll get your sister right away, Mr. Hardy," said Chief Collig, standing across the desk from Frank and Joe's father.

Fenton Hardy turned around. "Well, if it isn't the traveling twosome! Don't you think you could have saved your trip to New York until after we got your aunt out of trouble?"

"That's why we went to New York, Dad. To *get* her out of trouble."

Fenton Hardy's eyes narrowed. "Why don't you start by telling me exactly what happened?"

"Well, you see, we think someone is—" Frank started to say.

But he was cut off by Aunt Gertrude's voice, choked with emotion. "Oh, Fenton!" she exclaimed. "I'm so glad you're here!"

They turned to see Aunt Gertrude approaching Fenton with her arms outstretched. Beside her stood Officer Riley, the envelope of photos tucked under his arm.

Aunt Gertrude embraced Fenton and burst into tears. "I was nowhere *near* that pier, Fenton!"

"Of course you weren't, Gertrude," Fenton said reassuringly, patting her back. "Now, don't worry. I'll get to the bottom of this." He looked up at Officer Riley. "I'm sure you have an explanation for accusing my sister of the murder of Henry Simone, Con."

"Well, Fenton," Officer Riley replied with a sigh. "It's as strange to me as it is to you. But first I think you ought to look at these."

He handed Fenton Hardy the evidence and walked toward a demure, white-haired woman sitting quietly on a bench.

"Look at that, will you?" Aunt Gertrude said in a shaky voice, pointing toward the four photographs. "He thinks that's me in the pictures!"

"Funny, it does look a bit like you," Fenton Hardy said. "But even so . . ."

Officer Riley said a few words to the elderly woman, then slowly brought her over to the four Hardys. "Uh, pardon me, Miss Hardy," Officer Riley said, "but do you recognize this woman?"

Aunt Gertrude grew fidgety and forced a smile. "Why, yes, of course. Edna Sutter," she said. "From Saturday night bingo."

"Hello, Gertrude," Edna Sutter said in a sober, clipped voice.

"What brings you here, Edna?" Aunt Gertrude asked warily.

Before the woman could answer, Officer Riley said to her, "Mrs. Sutter, I'd like to repeat what you told me over the phone. Now, you read the newspaper account of the Simone murder. Is that correct?"

"Yes, sir," Edna said, jutting her chin out resolutely.

"And you remembered driving home with your husband late Sunday night—"

"That's right. We were returning from my grandson's birthday party up in Short Hills. He was six that day—no, seven—"

"That's wonderful, Mrs. Sutter. Congratulations. And what exactly did you see when you got back into Bayport?"

Edna Sutter's eyes darted back and forth between Aunt Gertrude and Officer Riley. "Well, the weather was lovely, so we decided to take the road along the pier. I was about to suggest to Philip—that's my husband—that we stop to take a walk—"

"But you didn't . . ." Officer Riley continued.

"Well, no. You see, there was already another couple out there, and they seemed to be having cross words with each other. Now, I thought it would be improper to intrude on their privacy. I remember noticing how handsome the man was, and then the woman's face struck me as being familiar. I said to myself, 'Edna, isn't that Gertrude from bingo?' Of course, I didn't think any more of it until I saw the picture of the murdered man in the newspaper the next day. Then I realized who he was—the fellow who was walking with Gertrude!"

She set her jaw and looked Officer Riley straight in the eye. "Of course, I thought it my civic duty to report this. It was just as we were saying at my last bridge club meeting: this society needs to be more vigilant—"

"Uh, thank you so much, Mrs. Sutter," Officer Riley interrupted. He helped her into her coat. "You've been a big help, and I'll be sure to call you when we need you again."

As Edna Sutter walked away, Fenton Hardy shook his head. "I wouldn't trust that lady with a—"

But at that moment Aunt Gertrude burst into

tears. "All right! All right! I've had enough!" she cried.

"What is it, Gertrude?" Fenton Hardy asked gently.

"I'll admit it! I lied!"

Gertrude Hardy lifted her tearstained face. "She was right. Cyril and I were on the pier!"

Chapter

12

GERTRUDE HARDY COLLAPSED into her brother's arms, her shoulders heaving. While she sobbed, Frank, Joe, and Fenton Hardy stood with their jaws open. Gertrude Hardy sounded like a broken woman about to confess to murder!

"And those people in the photo?" Fenton Hardy asked. "They are you and Simone, Gertrude?"

Aunt Gertrude nodded, wiping tears from her eyes. "Yes," she said softly. "But I can explain it all!"

Mr. Hardy put his arm around her and sat her down. "That's all right, Gertrude. Now, why don't you tell us exactly what happened—slowly, from the beginning." He gave her a handkerchief from his jacket pocket.

"I'm sorry, it's—it's just that the memories are so painful. . . ." Her voice was choked as she looked desperately from face to face. Then, shaking her head ruefully, she let out a big sigh and began her story.

"The night he was murdered, Cyril and I went for a walk along the pier. As Frank and Joe will tell you, the two of us were having rather rough times. He seemed to be such a kind, gentle man at first. I'd never—never fallen for anyone so quickly. I felt like a young girl again!" A smile flickered across Aunt Gertrude's face, but it quickly dissolved into a frown.

"Then suddenly he changed. He wouldn't show up for our dates, he stopped returning calls. I was so angry with him that I decided to confront him at his cottage."

"And this was Sunday night, the night that he was murdered?" Officer Riley asked.

"That's right. It was about—oh, nine-thirty, nine forty-five or so. I found him in the cottage, working. He'd completely forgotten about the date we'd made. He apologized and suggested we take a walk down Bay Road to the pier. But all the way there he just seemed so—so distant, so uncaring. By the time we got to the pier, I'm afraid I completely lost my temper."

"And, uh, what exactly happened when you lost your temper?" Officer Riley asked.

Aunt Gertrude shifted uncomfortably. "You

know, I've always been a peaceful, loving person. I've never done anything to hurt anyone—until that night. I—I guess I just lost control."

Frank was beginning to feel warm. He looked at Joe and his father and realized they were probably all thinking the same thing. Was Aunt Gertrude's "explanation" going to turn into a confession? Could she have done it after all?

"Before you go on, Gertrude," Officer Riley said, "remember, you have a right to remain silent and to have a lawyer present—"

"I slapped him."

A long, expectant silence stretched for several seconds. Finally Officer Riley looked at her blankly. "You—slapped him?"

"That's right. I think it shocked me more than it did him. Anyway, that's when we had our long talk, and we patched everything up."

"Then why did you leave by yourself?" Officer Riley asked, holding up the picture that seemed to show her walking away alone.

"I—I didn't. We left together," Aunt Gertrude replied. She took the picture and examined it pathetically. "I can't understand this. He and I were together the whole time."

"You're sure?" Officer Riley pressed.

Aunt Gertrude came back to life. "Of course I'm sure! Do you think I'm old and dotty? My memory is perfectly good!"

Officer Riley shifted uncomfortably from leg to

leg. "Well, Gertrude, it's just that this was the last time Simone was seen alive. Now I want you to think about that night—try to recall the anger you felt, and whether you had the knitting needle with you—"

"My knitting needle?" Aunt Gertrude laughed. "Oh, please, Officer Riley, why would I bring a knitting needle on a walk?"

Con Riley shook his head and sighed, looking at the photos. "I don't know, Miss Hardy, I just don't know."

"May I see those?" Frank asked. Officer Riley handed him the photos and Frank riffled through them. "As far as we can tell, these first few pictures *are* Aunt Gertrude and Simone. But this one . . ." He held up the photo of Aunt Gertrude walking away alone. "This one must be an impostor."

"How can you be so sure?" Con Riley asked.

"I start by assuming Aunt Gertrude is innocent. Not only because she's my aunt—"

"But because we're supposed to assume a person is innocent until *proven* guilty," Fenton Hardy said with a meaningful glance at Con Riley.

"Harrrrumph, yes, of course," Officer Riley replied.

"My theory," Frank went on, "is that someone is trying to frame her. We don't know who yet. Now, this last photo does resemble Aunt

Gertrude, but it's just fuzzy enough so that we can't tell for sure—"

Joe looked over his brother's shoulder. "Is there anything about the person that's different? Clothing? Hair? Anything?"

They all examined it closely. Frank tried to make out details, but the lighting was so dark, it was hard to tell.

"That dress could be any color," Aunt Gertrude said. "And the hair looks like mine, but for all I know it could be a wig."

"The lights along the pier are the same," Mr. Hardy said, scratching his chin. "If there were only some way to tell that these pictures were taken at different times, or on different days. . . ."

Joe scrutinized the photos carefully. "The same boats are in the water in each shot."

"And judging from the way they're reflecting the streetlights, they seem to be at the same level," Frank added. "That means the tides are about the same."

"Too bad the moon isn't in the photos," Fenton Hardy remarked. "We could check its shape and position."

Frank looked closely at the almost pitch-black skies. "This must be some film," he said. "It picked up every possible light source." He pointed to the stars, which showed up as tiny flecks of white. He flipped from photo to photo.

"Hmm," Frank said. "Same star formations in each one of these—"

Joe turned the last photo so he could see it better. He put his face close to it, squinting. "Except for the little dots in this one . . ."

"Probably a plane passing overhead," Frank suggested. Suddenly his face lit up. "That's it!" he exclaimed.

"What's it?" Aunt Gertrude asked.

Frank grabbed Aunt Gertrude's hand. "Aunt Gertrude, do you remember seeing or hearing a plane?"

"Well—no, I don't believe so," Aunt Gertrude answered. "But honestly, Frank, that's not the sort of thing that would stick in my mind."

"True," Frank said, a gleam in his eyes. "But if there was a flight that night, there would be a record of it at the Bayport/Barmet Airport!"

"Good point," Fenton Hardy said with a proud smile. "Can you get it for us, Con?"

"You bet," Officer Riley answered. He went over to the phone and punched the number. "Hello, this is Officer Con Riley, Bayport police. I need someone who handles the list of all flights in and out of the airport. Yes, hello, ma'am. I need to know all the flights into and out of the airport this past Sunday night. After twenty-one hundred hours, please." Officer Riley furrowed his brow. "Mm-hmm . . . Yes. . . . You're sure?"

"What's she saying?" Joe demanded.

"Just a second, ma'am." Officer Riley pressed the hold button. "No go. There were three flights—nine forty-two, ten oh-seven, ten twenty-three."

A look of disappointment washed across everyone's faces. Frank stared at the picture again, as if looking for inspiration.

Officer Riley put the phone to his mouth. "Okay, thank you for your help, ma'am. . . ."

"Wait!" Frank shouted before Officer Riley could hang up. He held up the picture and pointed to the water. "Ask her which flights had a pattern that took it over Barmet Bay."

Officer Riley asked her the question, grunted "mm-hmm" a couple of times, and hung up the phone. "All flights that night came in from the northwest." A wide smile grew across his face. "None of them had a traffic pattern that put them anywhere near the bay! According to the flight log, there was a flight over the bay on Monday night. Whoever took that picture had to have done it on Monday—the day *after* the murder."

"All riiiiight!" Joe yelled, giving a little punch in the air.

"Well," said Officer Riley with a smile, "this doesn't really prove anything. But it gives us cause to doubt. I'm going to allow you to go home *if* your brother will be responsible and post bail." Fenton Hardy nodded. "I apologize for the inconvenience."

Aunt Gertrude didn't say a word. But the warm hug she gave Mr. Hardy and the boys left no doubt how she felt.

Frank shrugged his shoulders. "That part was easy. Now all we have to do is figure out who took the picture—and who the impostor was."

Frank and Joe drove home in the van while Mr. Hardy took Aunt Gertrude in his car. They all arrived at the house at the same time to find the door locked and the answering machine blinking.

"That must be for one of you," Fenton Hardy said with a grin. "Everyone else thinks we're still away on vacation."

"Where's Mom?" Joe asked, looking around.

"Over at the Halperns," Fenton Hardy said. "They saw us come in and invited us to dinner." He looked at his watch. "To which I'm very late. Gertrude, do you want to come? I know you're welcome."

"No, Fenton, I just want to have a hot bath and sit in my own house and not move."

"See you!" With that, Fenton gave his sister a quick kiss and left.

Frank flicked on the answering machine's replay button. The first message was from Callie.

"Call me when you get in, Frank. I want to know how the day went—"

"So she can tell us how we could have done it better!" Joe said with a chuckle. The boys started walking into the kitchen, but the sound of the next message stopped them in their tracks.

"Hello, Frank and Joe. Justin Spears here. I'm calling to let you know I've come across some startling new information. I don't want to talk over the phone, so I'm having it carried to your house by messenger. He'll be on the three oh-five train to Bayport."

"Carried to our house?" Frank said. "I don't see any sign of—"

"Shhh!" Joe hissed. "The next message is Spears too!"

This time Spears sounded frantic. There was a slamming noise in the background, as if someone were trying to smash in a door. "You've got to get that briefcase—it may still be on the train! I— I don't have much time to talk. Listen closely. The stuff is crucial! It shows that—"

A sudden crash drowned out Spears's voice.

"Nooooo!" Spears screamed. "Let go— *grrrraggggh!*"

There was the *bonk* of a phone receiver clattering to the floor. Then all the Hardys could hear were fragmented sounds, like those of a struggle. Things crashing around and gasping, followed by what sounded like someone making horrible choking noises. Then came a dull thud, followed by silence.

Finally, with the cold click of the phone being replaced, the message came to an abrupt end.

Chapter

13

Joe slammed his hand down on the phone stand. "I don't believe this! Someone nailing Spears. And what is this about a briefcase?"

Frank yanked the handset off the phone and called New York City Information. "Justin Spears please—a business number." He thought for a moment. "The home phone, too, if you have one." Taking a pencil out of a holder, he wrote down the numbers.

He tried both numbers. No one answered at the office, and he had to leave an urgent message to call him on Spears's home phone machine.

"I don't like the feeling I'm getting," Frank said, replacing the handset. "He's probably lying on the floor of his office!"

Aunt Gertrude put a hand to her chest. "Oh,

my goodness," she exclaimed. "Do you really think something happened to him? What can we do?"

"Call the New York City police," Joe suggested.

Suddenly Aunt Gertrude groaned and clutched onto the side of the phone stand. "You know, this is getting to be too much for me. I'd like to lie down."

"I'll help you upstairs," Joe volunteered. He walked Aunt Gertrude to her room while Frank called the police.

By the time Joe came back downstairs, Frank was pacing back and forth. "The three oh-five . . ." Frank said, almost to himself. "That was the train *we* almost took."

"If only we'd known! Spears's messenger could have met us at the station."

Suddenly Frank's eyes widened. "Spears's messenger! Of course! Remember who we saw pushing his way out of the train as if his life depended on it?"

Immediately the image came back to Joe. "Bart," he said. "Spears's assistant! But why?"

"Because he really *did* feel as if his life depended on it! He recognized Fleckman's goons—they must have been the men who beat him up and trashed Spears's office. So he thought they were after him—or the contents of his briefcase!

Do you remember what he had with him as he came out of the train?''

Joe thought back. ''Nothing, I think.'' A look of realization came over his face. ''And that's why Spears called—because Bart left the briefcase on the train!''

''The important thing is that it might still be on that train, and we've got to find it!''

Joe looked at his watch. ''It's six already. The train goes only as far as Bridgefield. It's been there and gone.''

''Yeah, but they must have a lost and found . . .''

Frank was out the door before Joe could finish. He jumped into the front seat of the van. Within seconds Joe was next to him and they were on their way to Bridgefield.

''What if someone took it?'' Joe asked as they entered the ramp to the highway.

''Let's hope not,'' Frank answered. ''Maybe no one even noticed it.''

Joe looked ahead of them at the highway. ''Uh-oh,'' he mumbled.

''The last of rush hour!'' Frank grumbled as he pulled into a line of slow-moving cars. ''Just what we need.''

Frank moved into the left lane, where the traffic was moving the fastest—and that was still slightly more than a crawl.

They sat in frustrated silence for a few minutes, until Joe said, "I just can't figure it out."

"Which part?" Frank asked.

"The main one—who killed Simone. I mean, there are motives all over the place. It's clear that Fleckman might have done it. He did send his goons to kill us. But I'm not convinced Spears is completely innocent either. It seems hard to believe his story that Simone was almost broke when he died."

Frank nodded. "Maybe Fleckman was telling the truth about him. Maybe Simone really was an embezzler, and Spears is hiding his money."

"Not to mention Mrs. Simone. We haven't found any explanation for that scarf, and you said she didn't seem shocked or upset at the Shore Inn when you told her about Simone's death."

"Well, there was no reason for her to be surprised. I mean, I wasn't the first to tell her about his death—she'd already hired Elite Eye by the time I saw her."

"True," Joe admitted.

"What I can't figure out is who could have framed Aunt Gertrude! None of the suspects even knew her." Frank furrowed his brow with exasperation. "Something's missing."

The loose ends all jumbled together in Frank's mind: Fleckman's goons . . . Spears's phone call . . . those dark, grainy photos . . . Mrs. Simone and Clifton . . .

Clifton. Suddenly Frank's mind went back to the first time he'd met the detective. He thought about the scuffle in Simone's upstairs bedroom—and about a still-unanswered question he had.

The camera. The camera *without a flash*.

Frank's mind began to race. "Joe," he said in a voice taut with excitement. "Remember when I told you about the camera in Simone's bedroom?"

"Right," Joe answered with a smile. "The one that didn't have the flash."

"Obviously Clifton had set the camera up to photograph the cottage for clues. Now, a flash *is* great for indoors, but for close-ups, the light is too strong, and you're better off without it."

"Mm-hmm," Joe said, following the explanation. "But you need a lot of sunlight in the room, right?"

"Exactly. But that bedroom was shaded by trees—it was pretty dark in there."

"Well, he probably used some sort of super-high-speed film that can take pictures in the dark." Joe shrugged. "I mean, the pictures would be pretty grainy—"

Frank grinned. "And," he added, "if the film were used outdoors—say on a dark night—the images would be barely recognizable, wouldn't they?"

A look of sudden realization flashed across

Joe's face. "So *Clifton* took those photos at the pier!" he said in a hushed voice. "But how—"

"He must have been on the case *before* Mrs. Simone called him in. How else could he have taken a picture of Aunt Gertrude and Mr. Simone that night?"

Joe shot a baffled glance toward Frank. "But why would he frame Aunt Gertrude? Unless— Maybe he's working *very* seriously for Alexandra Simone—covering up a murder. That call!" he exclaimed.

Frank glanced over at him. "What call?"

"The call for Clifton at Mrs. Simone's place— the one she said was urgent. It could have come just after Spears was attacked trying to call us!"

A chilling image shot through Frank's mind— an image of some thug-for-hire talking into a phone receiver over Spears's unconscious body, telling Clifton exactly what Spears had said over the phone!

Frank gripped the steering wheel and abruptly swung to the right, straight over the slow lane and into the breakdown lane. "Hang on!" he yelled. "Unless we're very, very lucky, that evidence is probably in Clifton's hands right now!"

A crowd of passengers were spilling out of a train as Frank and Joe pulled up to the Bridgefield station. They got out of the van and looked around. Frank spotted the large hand-painted sign that said Lost and Found. "Bingo! There it is."

Behind the counter at the lost and found was a jovial man with half-glasses perched at the end of his nose. His stringy red hair was parted beside his ear and then combed up over his head to try to cover his baldness. Some of the strands fell loose and hung over his ear as he spoke to Frank and Joe.

"Let me guess, fellas," he said. "You're the ones who left the set of albums by Frontal Lobe on the four twenty-three—"

"Uh, no," Frank said. "Actually, we're here to see if there was anything left on the three oh-five."

The man scratched his head. "Don't know. Yes. Yes, there was. A tan briefcase, I believe."

"That's it!" Joe said. "We're picking it up for a Mr. Justin Spears."

"Be right back." The man whistled as he walked into a back room.

"We got it!" Joe said through clenched teeth, trying to hold back his excitement. "I guess we were wrong about Clifton."

But when the man came back, he was reading from a notepad in his hand. "Looks like Mr. Spears didn't trust you guys!" he said with a chuckle. "It seems he was by just moments ago to pick up his own briefcase."

"Wh-what?" Frank stammered. "That can't be!"

"Hmm, must've been that strange fella my co-worker took care of." He looked into the distance over the top of his glasses. "Well now, isn't that him outside, just over there!" He pointed out the window.

Frank and Joe wheeled around to see a man with dark goggles and helmet climb onto a motorcycle. He revved the engine, and with the tires squealing, he took off.

Tucked firmly under his arm was a tan leather briefcase.

Chapter

14

"HE MUST BE HEADING for the highway! Let's get him!" Joe shouted.

He and Frank ran to the van. This time Joe took the driver's seat. He threw the van into reverse and slammed out of the space.

Honnnnk! The bleat of a car horn made Joe screech to a sudden stop. He narrowly missed broadsiding a station wagon.

"Watch it, Joe!" Frank said. "A little less speed will get us there as fast."

Joe had slammed the van into first and spun on some gravel. They had careened toward a thick cement pole. Joe spun the wheel and sped to the exit to find ten motionless cars lined up ahead of them, waiting for a break in the traffic.

"Joe—" Frank said warningly.

"We're going to lose this guy if we don't do something!" Joe passed everyone by driving up on the curb. They entered traffic accompanied by a chorus of honking horns.

Even so, the cyclist had disappeared. "We blew it," Joe said in disgust.

"Okay, we blew it," Frank agreed. "But I've got another plan."

"Like what? This guy is probably halfway to Bayport by now!"

Frank reached for the cellular phone and punched a few numbers in, saying, "Okay, Callie, you wanted to be part of the action? Well, here goes—"

"Callie? Why—"

"She can drive over and wait for him by the entrance ramp. Then she can either tail him or stall him."

Callie said she would set off immediately. As Frank hung up the phone, Joe yanked the steering wheel to the left and sent the van swerving into an opening in the fast lane. "Okay, we're starting to move," he said.

Frank gripped his armrest as Joe jumped from lane to lane. "This might not be so bad after all," Joe said.

"Hey, calm down, Joe!" Frank interrupted. "The cops are out! All we need is to be stopped for reckless driving!"

Joe's eyes darted up ahead of them a quarter

of a mile, where a police car had stopped in the breakdown lane, its lights flashing. Joe slowed and stayed in one lane.

As they got nearer the police car, an officer was just climbing back into his cruiser. The person he had stopped was blocked from Frank and Joe's view by a tractor-trailer.

"Somebody probably trying to drive in the breakdown lane," Frank said. "Sound like a familiar trick?" he asked sheepishly.

Joe looked over to his brother and grinned. Out of the corner of his eye he saw the police car drive away. Then the tractor-trailer slowly moved ahead to reveal who the police officer had stopped.

A man standing beside a motorcycle, with a tan briefcase.

"There he is!" Joe said. "Go get the briefcase, Frank!"

Frank wasted no time. He pushed open the door and jumped out of the van.

Cars skidded to a stop and blew their horns as Frank darted between them. The motorcyclist glanced around and did a double-take. Then, tucking the briefcase under his arm, he mounted his bike and kicked it into action.

Frank was only inches behind him. "Oh, no, you don't—" he said, lunging for the briefcase.

But the only thing that Frank grabbed was a

handful of gravel. He landed face first on the road as the motorcycle roared off.

"Come on, get in!" came Joe's voice. The van was now beside Frank, in the right lane. Frank jumped through the open door, still shedding gravel. A few cars ahead of them, the motorcycle had pulled into the same lane.

"He's playing it safe," Joe said. "He doesn't want to get stopped again."

The motorcyclist dodged from lane to lane, trying to put distance between himself and the Hardys. But Joe skillfully swerved and dodged into spaces between cars.

Finally the motorcyclist pulled onto the dotted white line between the lanes. He sped up, driving with cars on his right and left.

Practically at the same time traffic ground to a dead halt. Angry drivers opened the doors of their cars and moved outside to see what had happened.

Joe punched the dashboard. "Another jam! We've lost him now!"

Frank watched hopelessly as the motorcyclist drew farther away. As he picked up speed, he gave a quick glance over his shoulder, as if to taunt the Hardys.

Thump! All of a sudden the motorcycle skidded to the left, swerving to avoid an open door on the right. The rider hit the car on the left and went flying onto the car's hood.

Frank and Joe watched as the briefcase hurtled into the air and made a crash landing on the ground.

Clutching his stomach, the motorcyclist rolled off the car hood. Frank and Joe both bolted out of the van and ran for the briefcase.

And at the same time, there was a screeching of tires in the traffic going in the opposite direction.

"Frank! Joe!" a familiar voice called out.

The brothers looked to their left. Cars going in the opposite direction were stopping to avoid a collision with a car that had halted in the fast lane—a car driven by Callie! Frank and Joe looked disbelievingly at her as she waved hello.

Around her, motorists blew their horns and screamed heatedly.

In that moment of distraction the motorcyclist had risen to his feet. Frank and Joe dove for the briefcase.

"Got it!" Frank grinned triumphantly as his fingers closed around the leather handle.

"Way to go!" Joe shouted.

Immediately they sprang to their feet, ready to do battle with the motorcyclist.

But he'd disappeared from in front of them. "Wha— Where'd he go?" Joe said, straining to see into the distance.

"*Yeeeeaaaagh!*" A scream rang out. Frank and Joe turned to their left.

There, where they had just seen Callie, was the motorcyclist, his arm firmly around Callie's neck!

"Don't try anything!" the man called in a gravelly voice, a snub-nosed automatic appearing in his other hand. "I'll use this if I have to." He backed up toward his motorcycle, which lay in the center of the road on the double yellow line.

As dozens of motorists stared dumbfounded, the motorcyclist looked at Frank and Joe from behind his dark goggles. Slowly he walked backward, clutching Callie.

"I'm backing up to my bike," he said. "And I expect to be met there by you two young gentlemen—with that briefcase. Understand?"

Frank and Joe hesitated. Immediately the motorcyclist tightened his grip on Callie's throat. She gagged and flailed with her arms, trying to break free.

"Of course, you don't have to listen to me," the man said with a demonic grin. "You can take the briefcase with you. But you'd better say a final goodbye to your little girlfriend—right now!"

Callie's eyes pleaded desperately. But as the man yanked her backward toward the bike, Frank stood, unmoving. With only seconds to decide what to do, Frank seemed to have become paralyzed.

Chapter

15

"FRANK! DO SOMETHING!" Joe whispered harshly.

Frank's eyes jumped to Callie. He tried to think of a scheme, a way to keep both the evidence and save Callie. But he realized there was no choice.

Slowly, he walked toward the motorcyclist, holding the briefcase out to him.

The motorcyclist stopped walking backward. "No bluffing, kid," he threatened. "Or you'll be sorry."

"No bluffing, Clifton," Frank said soberly. He held out the briefcase, but the cyclist made no move to take it. "How did you—"

"You gave yourself away," Frank told him. "Making the assumption that Callie was my girlfriend. A stranger would just as easily have paired her with Joe. But you met us before, at the Shore Inn. So you knew who she went with—and told me who you were, even in that biker disguise with the space helmet on.''

"Very clever—but I'm getting the evidence. Take it, Callie," Clifton told his prisoner. "You'll tote it for me." Maintaining his grip on her neck, with the gun still held against her, he continued walking backward.

"Hey! What about her?" Frank asked.

"Don't worry," Clifton said with a sadistic laugh. "You'll get her as soon as I get to my bike. Fair enough?"

Right then two sharp sounds cut through the air—like a pair of gunshots.

"Lying little—" Clifton fell to the ground, dragging Callie down with him. The motorists who had climbed out of their cars to watch now dove back inside them.

As they fell to the road, Callie managed to slip out of the loosened grip of her captor. Quickly, she rose to her knees, still holding the briefcase in her hand.

"Oh, no, you don't!" Clifton tripped Callie, grabbing for the briefcase handle with one hand. The gun in his other hand wavered, giving Frank his chance.

Frank lunged forward, snapping a karate kick that sent the pistol flying off. Callie took advantage of the moment to yank on the briefcase, trying to pull it free.

Clifton swung her around, sending her into Frank. Both Callie and Frank went tumbling backward, but Callie kept her death grip on the handle. With a snap the briefcase tore open, sending papers flying in the air around them.

Quickly Frank and Callie scrambled for the papers.

"Joe! Help us catch them!" Frank yelled.

"I'll do my best," Joe replied.

"Aaaaaaaagh!" came Clifton's voice.

Frank, Joe, and Callie looked up from their paper chase. Clifton was buckled over against the side of a truck, holding his stomach. Standing in front of him, fists clenched, was a thick-shouldered man wearing a T-shirt and work pants.

"Come on, you lousy coward!" the man was shouting. "You like terrorizing young girls? How about picking on someone your own size?"

The door to the truck's cab was wide open where the man had obviously just climbed out. Frank and Callie looked over to see that the truck had rolled over the motorcycle, twisting its body and flattening both its tires. Joe laughed. "So that's where we got those great sound effects! It really sounded like two gunshots, didn't it?"

A dull thud came from the front of the truck, and they turned to see the truck driver slumped against a car. Then, with a sharp, strong karate chop, Clifton struck the man's shoulder. The truck driver fell to the ground, helpless.

Joe grabbed the papers from Frank and Callie, stuffing most of them into the tan briefcase. "You guys run for Callie's car. I'll take care of this." Looking to his right, he knocked on the door of a small blue sports car nearby. "Help us out with this, will you?" he called.

The driver, a young, brown-haired woman in a silk blouse and pin-striped jacket, grinned and pushed open the rear door for Joe.

Meanwhile, Clifton rushed for Frank and Callie, trying to cut them off before they reached Callie's car. Frank whirled around, setting his feet in a karate stance.

The crooked detective tried to dart past, going for Callie. But Frank threw a low kick at him, moving to protect her. Pivoting on one leg, Clifton dodged, then sent a flashy high kick at Frank's face. While Frank blocked that, Clifton threw a fist to the side of his head.

Frank gave ground, realizing he might be outclassed. Clifton came on with a barrage of martial-arts blows and kicks while Frank blocked and backpedaled, unable to launch an attack of his own.

"Hit him, Frank! Let's get out of here!" Callie called out.

That distraction got Frank on the ground—sent there by a smash from Clifton's elbow. Groggily, he pushed himself up on one knee, expecting a deathblow. But Clifton had been distracted too.

The crackling sound of paper had caught his attention. He snapped his head around to see Joe frantically stuffing papers into a briefcase in a nearby car. A low chuckle escaped his mouth. "Divide and conquer, huh? Too bad it didn't work."

Nimbly, he made his way across the lanes of stalled cars as Frank stumbled after him, yelling, "Look out, Joe!"

But when Joe glanced up from the rear seat of the car, it was too late. Clifton had reached in through the open window to grab his neck.

"You ought to know better than to involve innocent people," he said. In the front seat the woman stared at him in fear.

"Give the guy what he wants," she said to Joe. "I don't want to get involved."

Joe reluctantly reached down to the seat beside him. "No monkey business!" Clifton warned. "I can snap your neck with this hold. Now, pass over Spears's briefcase, and don't try handing me that other one."

"You better believe you're not getting the other one," the woman said firmly. "It's mine."

Frank had a sick feeling in his gut as he staggered toward the car.

But Joe handed the briefcase through the window, shrugging helplessly to his brother.

In the distance a siren began to wail. Clifton looked up. "I was hoping to keep this," he said, snatching the briefcase. "But I guess I won't be able to." He glanced back at his destroyed motorcycle.

With fast, precise movements, he sprang into action. First he ran over to his bike and popped open the gas cap, which was now facing the ground. He placed his briefcase under it and let gasoline spill over it.

"He's going to destroy it!" Frank said. He started to sprint toward the man.

"No, Frank! Leave him!" Joe exclaimed.

There was something about Joe's voice—something insistent that made Frank pull himself back. He watched helplessly as Clifton walked to the shoulder and placed the soaked briefcase on a bed of gravel. Standing back from it, he lit a match and tossed it on top.

And with a loud whoosh the briefcase exploded into flames.

Frank felt anger welling up inside him—anger that they'd come so close to the evidence only to watch it burn before their eyes. But more than that, he was angry at his brother. For the first time he could remember, Joe had just given up. "What's gotten into you, Joe?" he snapped. "We've lost it now!"

Joe put his finger to his lips, signaling Frank to be quiet. He glanced up at Clifton.

"Go! Go!" the man was screaming to everyone around him. His face was lit up with a gloating, triumphant smile. "Show's over!"

Seconds later two police cars pulled up beside the detective, who was now looking at the charred remains of the briefcase and shaking his head.

"Okay, what's going on here?" a police officer said, stepping out of one of the cars.

By this time Callie had joined Frank and Joe. "Listen, I'm really sorry if I fouled things up, guys—"

Callie was cut off by the sound of a gruff voice. "You! The three of you! Over here!"

A police officer was signaling Frank, Joe, and Callie to the side of the road. Joe leaned over and whispered something to the woman in the blue sports car. She nodded eagerly.

As the traffic finally began to move again, the blue sports car pulled over onto the shoulder behind the police.

"Okay, you kids are coming with me," the officer barked.

"Wait a minute!" Frank said. "What's the charge?"

"This man explained how you knocked him off his motorcycle, wrecked it, spilled gasoline on his attaché case, and set it on fire."

Joe guffawed. "And what makes you think you should believe this creep?"

Clifton had now pulled off his helmet. "I knew they'd be trying to give me trouble, but I didn't know they'd have an accomplice."

As Frank and Joe started to protest, they were grabbed by two of the officers.

"Sorry we didn't catch them before things got out of hand, Mr. Clifton," the first officer said, looking down at a notepad. He shrugged his shoulders. "It's our fault. They match the descriptions you phoned in exactly."

Chapter

16

CLIFTON SMOOTHED BACK his hair and gave Frank and Joe a smug grin. "No problem, Officer Parnell, you did what you could. Too bad about the briefcase though. It contained some important papers regarding a case I was working on." He sighed.

"Are you going to press charges, Mr. Clifton?" Officer Parnell asked.

Clifton scratched his chin. "I don't think so. These two young men are trying to be detectives themselves. They bit off more than they could chew, trying to compete with me on this case. Now neither of us will know the answer—and they'll have to live with that. I think that's punishment enough." He gave the police officers a meaningful look. "You all look young. Let this be a lesson to you that professional jealousy doesn't pay."

During Clifton's speech Joe slowly inched back to the blue sports car. The brown-haired woman quietly reached into the back seat and handed him her briefcase.

"I don't know, Mr. Clifton," Officer Parnell said. "I think you're being awfully generous—"

Joe marched forward, the briefcase in his hand. "Doesn't surprise me," he said. "He can avoid publicity this way."

Clifton chuckled. "Yes. Publicity against you."

"No," Joe said with a confident smile. "Publicity that might make people suspect the truth— that you killed Henry Simone!"

Frank looked at Joe as if he were crazy. He knows better than to grasp at straws like that, Frank thought.

"Way to go, Joe!" Callie said.

"Well, well, you're impressing your friends, Joe," Clifton said. "But you realize that's a very serious accusation—not something to talk about foolishly."

"I know," Joe answered. He swung the briefcase around and pulled out a handful of papers. "And these are very serious pieces of evidence— and definitely not foolish."

Clifton laughed and turned toward the police officers. "I guess this is what you call playing private eye. I'm embarrassed to say I thought these boys were near-professional caliber.''

"Okay, pal," Officer Parnell said to Joe. "Give the lady back her papers.''

"Sorry," Joe replied. "I can't do that."

"What do you mean, you can't do that?" Officer Parnell was starting to become annoyed.

"Clifton burned them all." Joe's smile got bigger. "Except for the ones she needs. We put those under her car seat."

Clifton stared at him, his smile slowly fading.

"These are the papers Clifton wanted to burn." Joe held them out for everyone to see. Across the top of each one were the words Spears & Company, Certified Public Accountants.

"What? Th-those are— How—" Clifton stammered.

"I had a chance to skim over them while my new friend and I switched the contents of the briefcases." The brown-haired woman in the sports car beamed as Joe walked toward Clifton, reading from the papers. "I found it very educational. For instance, this sheet of paper right here—"

Frank, Callie, and the police officers gathered around Joe. On it was a picture of a young man with a full head of hair, a bushy mustache, a broken nose, and a defiant smile. His shirt was open at the neck to reveal a gold chain and medallion. Underneath the picture was the name

Edward "Cool Hand" Colson—and above it, the word Wanted.

"Now look closely," Joe said. "Add a couple of decades to this face. Imagine a receding hairline, a short haircut, some plastic surgery to fix that nose—"

"It's Clifton!" Frank said in amazement.

"Eddie Colson—" Officer Parnell said, thinking back. "The leader of the Cool Hand's Crew, that New York gang that used to do the dirty work for the Mob. The Organized Crime Strike Force busted up the gang, but when they went to arrest Colson, he'd disappeared."

"Yeah, and nobody heard about him for years!" another officer added. "I remember all the rumors: he'd died, he'd skipped the country and was living it up in Mexico . . ."

"Well, gentlemen, it seems you're looking at him now," Joe said. "And judging from the rest of the evidence in this briefcase, the Cool Hand's Crew is still alive. Only now it's called the Elite Eye detective agency!"

"This—this is outrageous! I'll sue you for slander—" Clifton bellowed.

"Fine," Joe said. "But you'll be doing it from a jail cell."

Clifton furiously pointed a finger at Joe. "You can't prove a thing!"

"Maybe I can't, but someone else can—someone who isn't alive anymore, thanks to you.

Someone who worked in a respectable investment firm, who could take all your illegal money and hide it. Someone with whom you enjoyed a long business relationship, until you suspected him of skimming money off the top!''

"I don't know what you're talking about!" Clifton said, his face crimson with rage.

"Oh, no? Does the name Henry Simone ring a bell? Because you'll be hearing his voice a lot in court—and yours too. It seems Simone used to like to tape his phone conversations.''

Joe held up a set of cassette tapes. "I bet these will make interesting listening. And then there's this—" He held up a letter, handwritten on stationery with the letter *S* on top.

"It's from Simone to Spears, a last-ditch cry for help. It seems that in the last few days of his life, after your little business arrangement went sour, Simone began to suspect that you were coming after him.''

"Coming after him?" Clifton exclaimed. "I don't know what you're talking about.''

"I'm talking about how Simone's clerk was murdered by mistake. Henry Simone realized he had to move fast. Spears was the only person he trusted, so every day after-hours he'd sneak into the city—"

"That's when he started missing dates with Aunt Gertrude," Frank said under his breath to Callie.

"In the darkness of his empty office at Thompson Welles, he assembled his evidence against Elite Eye, which he finally messengered to Spears on Saturday. The next night Simone was murdered!"

"I—I—" Clifton sputtered.

"Running out of gas, Cool Hand?" Joe said. "Don't worry, you'll have plenty of time to rest where you're going!"

Clifton lunged for Joe, but two of the police officers grabbed him. With a solid metallic click, Officer Parnell slapped handcuffs on Clifton and read him his rights.

At the same time, a hand suddenly grabbed Joe by the wrist. With a jolt he spun around.

"Easy!" a laughing voice said. Joe looked around to see the brown-haired woman from the sports car. "This was a lot of fun, but, uh—would you mind giving me back my briefcase?"

"Oh! Of course!" Joe answered. He took all the papers out of the briefcase and handed it to her. As she grabbed it, a business card fell out onto the road.

Out of the corner of his eye Joe saw it fall. He stopped to pick it up. "That's funny. I thought we took all of these out." He handed it to her. "Here."

"Keep it," the woman said. And as she climbed into her car and put it into gear, she gave Joe a wink and a smile.

Eric Clifton left, too—except he went in the back of a police car.

"Come here! Look—there they are!" Aunt Gertrude called out. Frank, Joe, Callie, and Fenton and Laura Hardy gathered around the TV set.

Aunt Gertrude burst into applause as the metropolitan news segment showed Clifton, Bruno, and Alexandra Simone being led into the jailhouse. As they passed the TV cameras, they hid their faces under their jackets.

"So tell me again," Fenton Hardy said. "How exactly was Mrs. Simone involved in this?"

"Well," Frank said, "*she* was the reason Simone chose Bayport as his escape spot. He thought he could win her back—that he could charm her into coming along with him to Europe to retire on his stolen money."

"And he was a real charmer." Joe picked up the story. "He got Alexandra Simone to meet with him in his cottage. But she found Aunt Gertrude's knitting stuff and realized he'd been seeing another woman. While they were arguing over that, Clifton and Bruno barged in."

"They just turned up?" Fenton Hardy asked.

Joe shook his head. "They must have known he was in the area and had been searching for him. Clifton and Bruno snapped pictures of Aunt Gertrude and Simone walking on the pier earlier, and probably tailed Simone to the cottage. Then

Mrs. Simone turned up—proof that they had the right man. So they came in after her. Simone tried to fight, grabbing the only weapon at hand—the knitting needle."

Aunt Gertrude closed her eyes. "It didn't seem to do him much good," she said quietly.

"They were ready to get rid of Mrs. Simone, too, but she promised to help them find the money Simone had embezzled. But first they had to cover the murder." Joe patted Aunt Gertrude on the shoulder. "I guess you were the perfect candidate for a frame-up."

"Meanwhile, Mrs. Simone led Clifton to Justin Spears," Frank explained. "She knew he'd been helping to hide some of Simone's shady deals. So he had to know where the money was."

"Spears wasn't about to give up all those big bucks though," Joe said.

"So it became like a treasure hunt," Fenton Hardy said. "Spears trying to hide the money, Clifton and Mrs. Simone looking for it."

"But there was a third player," Frank put in. "Henry Fleckman. Spears used Fleckman's account to move the money around and to set up a patsy for Clifton or anyone else investigating Simone's crooked deals. Fleckman wasn't going to take that rap. But he did want to take the money."

"But why would he try to kill *you?*" Fenton Hardy asked. "There was no reason."

"He probably just panicked. Anyway, Spears wound up getting double-teamed," Joe said. "Fleckman's goons roughed up Spears's assistant, but it was Clifton's people who finally killed Spears. Mrs. Simone had them stake out his office and wiretap his phone. That's how they found out about the evidence he was sending us. They killed him and phoned Clifton that the evidence was on the train—and you know the rest."

"Except, of course, Fleckman and his four goons are in the can awaiting trial for attempted murder—among other things," Frank said.

"Amazing," Mr. Hardy said. "You boys did a terrific job."

Aunt Gertrude looked skeptical. "Well, I don't know if I'd say that. *I'm* still out fifty grand!"

Joe shook his head grimly. "I guess Simone needed cash for his getaway. But it hasn't turned up. I guess Mrs. Simone could tell us something. She mentioned the cash in her testimony, but it's hardly a solid lead."

"What did she say?" Frank asked.

"Oh, just something about Simone saying he hid the money with no sweat—"

Suddenly Aunt Gertrude bolted up from her chair. *"No Sweat!* Frank, Joe! Drive me to the police station right away!"

"Why?" Joe asked.

"Don't ask questions, young man! Just do it!"

Fenton Hardy gave his sons a stern look, and they took Aunt Gertrude out to the van.

Minutes later they were at the station house. Aunt Gertrude charged up the stairs and burst through the front door.

"Buy low, sell high! Make a killing in the market! No sweat! Squawwwwk!" the parrot screamed back in the lounge, where he was still being kept until a new owner could be found.

Aunt Gertrude went straight to the cage and opened it.

"Dinnertime! Birdseed! No sweat!"

"I don't believe this," Joe muttered to Frank. "She wants to feed the bird."

"Atta boy, No Sweat," Aunt Gertrude said calmly. The parrot fluttered its wings as Aunt Gertrude examined the bottom of the cage. Then, carefully, she lifted a piece of loose cardboard, and the whole floor of the cage came up.

Underneath it, in flat bundles, were five groups of ten crisp thousand-dollar bills.

"Invest with confidence! *Braawwwk!*"

"Thank you, No Sweat!" Aunt Gertrude said with a smile. "This time I will take that advice."

Frank's and Joe's faces were covered with astounded grins. *"All riiiiiight,* Aunt Gertrude!" Joe said.

"Not bad for someone who hates detective work!" Frank added.

Aunt Gertrude shrugged as she put the money

into her pocketbook. "I only said I hate for you boys to do it." She held herself tall as she walked out past the front desk to the front door, a sly smile creeping across her face. "I don't mind when it's done *right!*"

"Oooh, that hurts," Joe said as Aunt Gertrude stepped outside.

Frank hesitated before going outside. "I don't know, Joe," he said. "Does this mean we have to send her out on cases from now on?"

Joe winced. Then he thought about it for a second and laughed. "Well, why not? Then you and I can stay home and cook for her."

From outside came the honking of the van's horn. "Hurry up, boys! My lasagna is going to get overdone!"

Frank turned to Joe. "Uh, on second thought," Frank said, "let's keep things just the way they are!"

"Coming, Aunt Gertrude!" Joe called out. And with a couple of wild whoops, the Hardy brothers raced each other to the van.

Frank and Joe's next case:

Callie Shaw, Frank's girlfriend, is away at UCLA taking a video course. When she phones pleading for help, both Hardys fly to California—but Callie has disappeared! It seems she has footage of a policeman beating a street person called Patch, and now the cop's out to get her—and the tape.

With the help of street people, Frank and Joe locate Callie. Then they search Patch's shack. There they find old newspaper clippings about a ten-million-dollar heist where the money was never recovered. The brothers and Callie dig deeper, their investigation leading them to a prestigious movie studio and to a star-studded Hollywood party, where they make a horrifying discovery. When the old-time criminal sets his dogs on the trio, will Callie's video camera be protection enough? Find out in *Nightmare in Angel City*, Case #19 in The Hardy Boys Casefiles™.

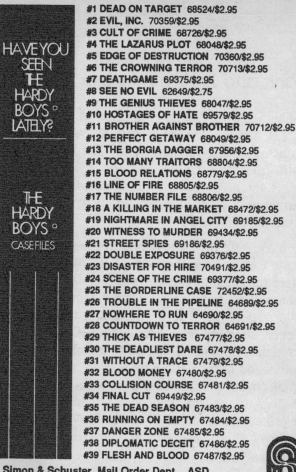